"A storyteller

Ambrose Bier

"Funny, compulsive . . . enjoyably raffish."   —*Esquire*

"Lansdale has a zest for storytelling and a gimlet eye
for detail."   —*Entertainment Weekly*

"A master at taking a simple everyday event and
turning reality upside down."   —*Mystery Scene*

"Lansdale is a storyteller in the Texas tradition of
outrageousness . . . but amped up to about 100,000
watts."   —*Houston Chronicle*

"When he's good, Lansdale is the best."
                          —*Rocky Mountain News*

"A cross between Robert B. Parker and Stephen King."
                          —*San Jose Mercury News*

Joe R. Lansdale

Savage Season

Joe R. Lansdale is the author of more than a dozen novels, including *Sunset and Sawdust* and *Leather Maiden*. He has received the British Fantasy Award, the American Mystery Award, the Edgar Award, the Grinzane Cavour Prize for Literature, and seven Bram Stoker Awards. He lives with his family in Nacogdoches, Texas.

www.joerlansdale.com

BOOKS BY JOE R. LANSDALE

In the Hap and Leonard Series

Savage Season
Mucho Mojo
The Two-Bear Mambo
Bad Chili
Rumble Tumble
Captains Outrageous
Vanilla Ride

Other Novels

Sunset and Sawdust
Lost Echoes
Leather Maiden

Savage Season

Savage Season

A Hap and Leonard Novel

JOE R. LANSDALE

VINTAGE CRIME/BLACK LIZARD
Vintage Books
A Division of Random House, Inc.
New York

FIRST VINTAGE CRIME/BLACK LIZARD EDITION, JANUARY 2009

Copyright © 1990 by Joe R. Lansdale

The Cataloging-in-Publication Data for *Savage Season* is on file at
the Library of Congress.

Vintage ISBN: 978-0-307-45538-3

www.vintagebooks.com

Printed in the United States of America
10 9 8 7

This is for Jeff Banks, dedicated with friendship.

"A great deal of intelligence can be invested in ignorance when the need for illusion is deep."

Saul Bellow

"Put all your eggs in one basket and—WATCH THAT BASKET."

Mark Twain, *Pudd'nhead Wilson*

Savage Season

1

I was out back of the house in the big field with my good friend Leonard Pine the afternoon it started. Me with the twelve gauge and him pulling the birds.

"Pull," I said, and Leonard did, and another clay bird took to the sky and I jerked the gun up and cut it down.

"Man," Leonard said, "don't you ever miss?"

"Just on purpose."

I'd switched to clay birds in favor of the real ones a long time back. I didn't like to kill anything now, but I still enjoyed the shooting. Getting the bead on something and pulling the trigger and feeling the kick on my shoulder and watching the target blow apart had its own special satisfaction.

"Got to open another box," Leonard said. "The pigeons are all dead."

"I'll load, you shoot for a while."

"I shot twice as long as you did and I missed half those little boogers."

"I don't care. My eye's getting off anyway."

"Bullshit."

Leonard got up, brushed his big black hands on his khaki pants, and came over and took the twelve gauge. He was about to load it and I was about to load the launcher, when Trudy came around the side of the house.

We both saw her about the same time. I turned to open another box of clay birds, and Leonard turned to pick up a box of shells, and she was swinging our way in the sunlight.

"Shit," Leonard said. "Here comes trouble."

Trudy was about four years younger than me, thirty-six, but she still looked twenty-six. Had that long blond hair and legs that began at the throat—good legs that were full at the thighs and dark of skin. And she knew how to use them, had that kind of walk that worked the hips and gave her breasts that nice little bounce that'll make a man run his car off the road for a look. She had on a tight beige sweater that showed she still didn't need a bra, and a short black skirt that was the current fashion, and it made me think of the late sixties and her mini-skirt days—back when I met her and she was going to be a great artist and I was going to find some way to save the world.

Far as I knew, closest she'd gotten to art was a drafting table and dressing mannequins in store windows, and the closest I'd gotten to saving the world was my name on some petitions, for everything from recycling aluminum cans to saving the whales. I put my cans in the trash now, and I didn't know how the whales were doing.

"Watch her," Leonard said, before she was in earshot.

"I'm watching."

"You know what I mean. Don't come crying over to my place if she does it to you again. Mind what I'm saying, now."

"I know what you're saying."

"Uh-huh, and a hard dick knows no conscience."

"It isn't that way and you know it."

"Well, it's some kind of way."

Now that Trudy was closer, the midday sun fell full on her face, I could see she didn't quite look twenty-six. The pores in her nose were a little larger and there were crows feet around her eyes and laugh lines at the corners of her mouth. She always had liked to laugh, and she'd laugh at anything. I remembered best how she laughed when she was happy in bed. She had a laugh then that was pretty as the song of a bird. It was the kind of thing I didn't want to remember, but the memory was there just the same, like a thorn in the back of my brain.

She smiled at us then, and I felt the January day become a little warmer. She could do that to a man, and she knew it. Liberated or not, she didn't fight that ability.

"Hello, Hap," she said.

"Hello," I said.

"Leonard," she said.

"Trudy," Leonard said.

"What're you boys up to?"

"Shooting some skeet," I said. "Want to shoot some?"

"Sure."

Leonard handed me the shotgun. "I got to go, Hap. I'll check you later. Remember what I told you, huh?"

I looked at that hard face of his, black as a prune, said, "Sure, I'll remember."

"Un-huh. See you, Trudy," and he went away then, making deep strides across the pasture toward the house where his car was parked.

"What was that all about?" Trudy said. "He seemed kind of mad."

"He doesn't like you."

"Oh yeah, I forgot."

"No you didn't."

"Okay, I didn't."

"You want to shoot first?"

"I think I'd really rather go in the house and have a cup of coffee. It's kind of chilly out here."

"You're not dressed like it's chilly."

"I've got hose on. They're warmer than you think. Just not warm enough. Besides, I haven't seen you in a while—"

"Almost two years."

"—and I wanted to look good."

"You do."

"So do you. You could gain a few pounds, but you look good."

"Well, you don't need to gain or lose an ounce. You look great."

"Jazzercise. I've got a record and I do what it says. Us older ladies have to work at it."

I smiled. "Okay, older lady. Why don't you help me gather this stuff, and we'll go on up to the house."

■ ■ ■ ■

She sat at the kitchen table and smiled at me and made small talk. I got down the coffee and tried to keep my mind off how it used to be between us, but I wasn't any good at it.

When I had the coffee maker going, I sat at the table across from her. It was slightly warm in the kitchen from the gas heaters, and close enough I could smell the scent of her minty soap and the hint of some perfume, probably dabbed behind the ears and knees and below her belly button. That's the way she used to do it, and the thought of it made me weak.

"Still working in the rose fields?" she asked.

"We've been digging them, but not for the last few days. The man me and Leonard work for is through with that part. It'll be a few days before he'll need us for anything else."

She nodded, ran one long-nailed hand through her hair, and I saw the glint of a small, gold loop in her earlobe. I don't know what it was about that gesture, about the wink of gold, but it made me want to take her in my arms, pull her on the table and make the two-year absence of her blow away.

Instead I contented myself with a memory, one of my favorites. It was about the time we went to this dance and she had worn this zebra-stripped blouse and mini-skirt. I was twenty-three and she was nineteen. The way she danced, the way she moved when she wasn't dancing, the smell of her, had made me manic with lust.

I had whispered something to her and she had laughed and we had gone out to my Chevy and driven to our favorite parking place on a pine-covered hill. I stripped her and she stripped me, and we made slow, sweet love on the motor-warm hood of my car, the moon shining down on us like a personal love-light, the cool summer breeze blowing across us like a feathered fan.

And the thing I remember best about that time, other than the act of copulation, was I had felt so goddamn strong and immortal. Old age and death were as wild and improbable as some drunken story about walking across the face of a star.

"How's . . . what is it? Howard?" It wasn't a thing I really wanted to ask, but it came out anyway.

"Okay. We're divorced. Have been for a year now. I don't

think I'm cut out for marriage. I had you and I screwed that up, didn't I?"

"No great loss."

"I left you for Pete and Pete for Bill and Bill for Howard. None of them worked out, and neither did the ones I didn't marry along the way. None of them came close to what we had. And the kind of men that are anything like you are harder and harder to find."

The flattery was a little thick, so I didn't have anything to say to it. I checked the coffee, poured a couple of cups. When I sat hers on the table, she looked at me, and I started to say something brotherly, but it wouldn't come out.

"I've missed you, Hap," she said. "I really have."

I put my coffee cup on the table next to hers and she stood and I held her and we kissed. The earth didn't move and my heart didn't stop, but it was quite all right just the same.

Then we had our hands all over each other, and we started moving toward the bedroom, molting clothes along the way. Under the covers we danced the good, slow dance, and she let loose with that laugh I loved so much, the one as sweet and happy as the song of a bird.

And I did not care to remember then that even the most predatory of birds, the shrike, can sing.

2

About two in the morning the phone rang. I got up, and went to the kitchen to answer it. I don't think Trudy even heard it.

It was Leonard.

"That bitch there?"

"Yeah."

"Shit. You're fucked again."

"It's different this time. I'm only getting laid. Remember what you said about a hard dick not knowing a conscience? You were right."

"Bullshit, don't give me that macho crap. I was just talking that way. You don't think like that and you know it. It's always got to be something to you. This is Leonard you're talking to here, Mr. Hap Collins, not some rose field nigger."

"Leonard, you *are* a rose field nigger, and so am I. I'm a white version."

"You know what I mean."

"What are you doing up at two in the morning minding my business?"

"Drinking, goddammit. Trying to get drunk."

"How are you doing?"

"I'd rate it about a five on a one-to-ten scale."

"Is that Hank Williams I hear in the background?"

"Not his ownself, but yes. *'Setting the Woods On Fire.'*"

"What key's he singing in?"

"You're not as funny as you think, Hap. Shit, I wish that whore wouldn't come around."

"Don't call her that."

"That's what she is. She comes around and you start to act funny."

"How funny do I get?"

"All moon-eyed and puppylike, talking about the good old days, giving me that self-righteous sixties stuff. I was there, buddy, and it was just the eighties with tie-dyed Tee-shirts."

"You numb nuts, you talk about the sixties just as much as I do."

"But I hated them. Shit, man, Trudy gets you all out of perspective. She gets to telling you how it was and how it ought to be now, and you get to believing her. I like you cynical. It's closer to the ground. I tell you, that bitch will say anything to get her way. She's fake as pro-wrestling. She's out there on a limb, brother, and she's inviting you out there with her. When the limb cracks, you're both gonna bust your ass. Get down from the tree, Hap."

"She's all right, Leonard."

"In the sack, maybe. In the head, uh-uh."

"No, she's all right."

"Sure, and wow, the sixties, man, like neat."

"This time is different."

"And next time I shit it'll come out in sweet-smelling little squares. Goodnight, you dumb sonofabitch."

He hung up, and I went over and got a glass out of the cabinet, filled it with water, drank it, leaned my naked rear into the counter and thought about things. What I thought about mostly was how cold it was.

I went back to the bedroom to get my robe, and looked down at Trudy. There was enough moonlight that I could see her face. The blanket had fallen off of her and she was lying on her side with her arms cuddling her pillow. I could see a smooth shoulder, the shape of one fine breast and the curve of her hip. Looked too innocent to have been the one in my bed a short time ago, screaming and groaning, and finally singing like a bird.

But she didn't look so innocent I wasn't stirred. I thought

about waking her, but didn't. I covered her gently, got my robe off the bedpost, went back into the kitchen and filled my glass with water again, took a chair at the table across from the window and looked out. With the curtains pulled back like they were, I could see the moonlit field where Leonard and I had shot skeet, could see the line of pines behind it, looking oddly enough like the outline of a distant mountain range.

I sat there and drank my water and thought about things, thought about Trudy and the sixties and what Leonard had said, and knew he was right. Last time she had come around and gone away, I had started on a monumental drunk that embarrassed the winos down at the highway mission, which was where Leonard found me—three months later. I had no idea where I had gotten the money for liquor, and I didn't know how much I'd drunk, couldn't even remember having started.

Since that time I had sworn off. Trudy, not the liquor. But now she was in my house again, in my bed, and I was thinking about her, considering all the wrong things, knowing full well I had fallen off the wagon again.

Until it had gone wrong between us (and it was a mystery to me as to when and how), our relationship had been as beautiful as a dream. And there were times when I felt it might have been just that.

We met at LaBorde University. I had made a late start due to no money and lots of hard work at the iron foundry trying to get me some. The foundry was a hot, horrible job where you wore a hard hat, watched sparks jump and heard the clang of steel pipe all day.

But it was money, and I thought it would allow me to go to college, get some kind of degree and find a way to make an easier living than my old man had; a way for me to get my slice of the American Dream.

Pretty soon I was wrapped up in the learning, though, and not for what it could get me financially. There was something in the books and lectures that went beyond the sports page and the martial arts I practiced, the color article section of the *TV Guide*. There was more to life than a beer with the buddies, a gold watch and a pension. It was the sixties, a time of love and peace and social upheaval—contradictions that walked side by side. Women's rights.

Civil rights. The Vietnam War. I got it in my head I could do some good out there, make things better for the underprivileged. I changed my major from business to sociology and went to anti-war rallies and sang some folk songs, collected Beatles albums, and let my hair grow long.

At one rally held at a Unitarian church, I met Trudy. I looked across the heads of long, straight hair and Afros and saw her on the other side of the room talking to a pear shaped girl in a flowered dress that belled and dragged the floor.

God, but Trudy was beautiful. Painfully young, a prototype for Eve. Long gold hair rippled to her waist and her eyes were so bright green they looked supernatural. Spangles of silver hung from her ears. She was wearing a white midi-blouse, a blue jean mini-skirt and wooden clog shoes. Beneath the midi was flat brown stomach and a marvelous belly button, and beneath the mini were legs like God would have given his very own woman.

I got over there without running and introduced myself. We made shameless small talk, mostly stupid mumblings, some of it about the war.

Pretty soon we had our arms around each other and we were out of there. We both lived in dorms then, and as the dorm mothers were furiously against fucking, I took her to a parking place that was to become our haven, and we did what we had wanted to do since the first moment we laid eyes on one another. We generated so much electricity upon that pine-covered hill, I'm surprised we didn't cause a forest fire. I feel certain we didn't do the shocks in my old Chevy much good.

This went on for a time, and things got better and hotter. And on the night of my fondest memory, when she wore the zebra-striped outfit, we decided to rent an apartment and move in together.

We pooled our money and found a little room on the grubby side of town and lived there for two months. It got better yet, and we decided to get married. It was a simple wedding with lots of flowers and barefoot guests and a female minister younger than Trudy.

God, those were odd times. If you missed them, and you know someone who went through them, soaked it all in, and you catch them late at night, after maybe a beer or two, or the kids are all in bed and the TV's dead, and you say, "Hey, what were the sixties really like?" There's a good chance they'll say "It was magical," or "It was special."

For a time it sure seemed that way. Peace and love seemed like more than words. We thought everyone could live in a world full of mutual respect, long hair, and cooperation. It was as if the sky had split open and God had given us a ray of light, and in its glow, wonderful things happened.

An example being the sparrow incident the night after our wedding.

We dropped the apartment and rented a small house on the edge of town. It wasn't much of a house. The ceiling in the living room was too low and the plumbing squeaked like giant mice.

Trudy turned on the back porch light and went out there to toss some potato peels, and found a sparrow sitting on the porch. It was weak and nodding and couldn't fly. She called me and I looked at it. It was a baby, and as far as I could determine, there were no wounds on it. It seemed sick.

I picked up the bird with some reluctance, because I had once been told if birds smelled the human scent on another bird they would peck it to death, and carried it into the house. I got an old shoebox and tore some newspaper up and put it in the bottom of the box and the bird on that. I got an eyedropper and used it to give the bird some cold beef bouillon.

That was the procedure from then on. First thing in the morning, and between classes, we would give the bird bouillon and clean its box and put fresh paper in the bottom. At night we stood over it and looked at it and clucked our tongues like parents worried about a sick child.

About this same time, I went to work part time in a restaurant in LaBorde, and brought home scraps I thought the bird might eat. At first he wouldn't touch them, but after a while he ate them out of my hand. Noodles were his favorite. I suppose they were as close as he ever got to worms.

The bird got stronger. He started flying around the house. You could open doors and windows and he wouldn't fly out. He liked it in there. He liked us. He'd light on our shoulders and our outstretched palms. He cheeped a lot, and because of that, we named him Cheep. The only time he showed distress was when we weren't wearing black. Guess because I had on a black Tee-shirt and Trudy a black peasant dress the night we found him, and he bonded to black.

We were so excited about our bird, we dyed everything we owned black. On those occasions when we did buy new clothes, they were always black. That way Cheep stayed happy.

Sweet alchemy was thicker in the air than radio waves then, and it seemed especially thick around Trudy and me. We thought it would last forever.

But even the best looking apple can contain a worm.

When 1970 rolled in just a few weeks after we were married, the Vietnam War still raged on. The relatively innocent smoking of grass had been exchanged by many for pills and shit-filled needles. The wonderful, if admittedly hokey, beauty of Woodstock had to stand shoulder to shoulder with the senseless tragedy at Kent State.

Our bird continued to fly about the house, but the magic of the era was gone. A deep, dark awareness that perhaps it had never actually existed settled in; we had glimpsed some shopworn cards up the magician's sleeve, and with each passing moment, the glow of the act was dimming.

The sixties were dead. They may never have lived.

I began to feel guilty about hiding out in college with my deferment when so many were dying in Vietnam. Asking that everyone be peaceful and love one another wasn't enough. I wanted to make some statement against the war, and I didn't want to hide behind a deferment to do it. I was one of those who felt our original cause in Vietnam was just, but that it had become a political nightmare. The government we were defending, in spite of cries of "We are a democracy," showed little evidence of being different from the one we were fighting. Our role there was as aimless as the flying Dutchman. We took a hill, we gave it back. The American dead stacked up. Seemed to me, we ought to have known when to cut our losses.

I talked to Trudy long and hard, and it was the sort of thing she loved. Noble involvement. It lit her like a torch.

With her blessing, I decided to quit college and allow myself to be drafted. When it came time to step forward and take the induction, I would refuse. I'd go the prison route instead. That would be my statement.

This was the time of the lottery, and I was drafted almost immediately. I was disappointed my draft notice didn't say *Greetings.* I had always heard that it did.

I went to Dallas, took my physical, passed, and refused to go.

The army tried to give me outs. I give them that. One officer even suggested I make a break for Canada. The war had soured even his way of thinking, and he was a lifer.

But I refused to run.

It was suggested I sign as a conscientious objector, but again I refused. C.O. status meant you thought fighting for anything, even your life, was wrong. I didn't believe that. Had I been around during the fighting of World War I or II, I would have gone and done my bit. The causes were just and the wars were fought with a conclusion in mind. I was an idealist, not a coward.

So I went to Leavenworth. Trudy and some of her friends came to see me from time to time and told me "right on" and how brave I was, and it felt good to hear it. They wrote me nice letters.

But that good feeling didn't last. It didn't relax me at night when I could hear the cons snorting and coughing and crying and farting and sodomizing each other. And there were guys in there who had bludgeoned their grandmothers to death who thought it their patriotic duty to kill me for not signing up to shoot gooks. If I hadn't been a pretty tough country boy with iron foundry muscles, I might not have made it.

Trudy kept coming to see me, but her friends dropped off. She kept writing, but the friends quit. She sent me clippings in her letters that told me what was going on outside, about the causes being fought for, the ground gained, the ground lost.

Then her visits thinned, and finally stopped. Next to last letter I got from her went on about how brave I was again and compared me to a number of counterculture heroes. It said Cheep had died and had been buried in a cream corn can out back of the house, and that she had met a man named Pete who was big in the ecology movement and they had this thing going. The last letter told me that the thing she and Pete had going was now really going, and she was filing for divorce. Nothing personal. She thought I was the bravest man she knew. It was signed like all the others: *Love Trudy.*

I did my time. Eighteen months altogether. I had planned

the day they let me out for a long time. I thought I would come out on a bright warm day with my fist held high, and Trudy would be there looking sexy and soft in a short wind-blown dress that would give me a good view of her long brown legs, and as the music came up, sweet but triumphant, she would run to me with those legs flashing and give me a kiss that would knock me silly from head to toes. Then she would load me in a car and drive us away.

But when I came out it was cold and drizzling. I had to talk a guard into calling someone to drive me to the bus station. Between paying for the car and the bus, the money I had when I went in and the money the government gave me for the nonstimulating manual labor I did inside was almost gone. Needless to say, I didn't feel like raising my fist.

I went back to East Texas and found out I didn't want to help the underprivileged anymore. I realized I was one of them. I got a job in the rose fields outside of LaBorde, and that's where I met Leonard. He was a Vietnam vet and a certified hardhead. He didn't like my views on a lot of things, but he didn't hold them against me either; I gave him someone to argue with. He was a martial artist, boxing, kenpo, hapkido, and he revived my interest. When I was in high school, until the time I met Trudy, I had been heavily involved in that sort of thing. Guess I dropped it later because I didn't feel it fit my new peace and love image or something. Anyway, I had been away for a time. I was glad to get at it again. I got better than ever before. It helped me work out some frustrations.

After a while, Trudy started coming around, and each time she went away she left me a bigger wreck than before. Built me up with promises, then left me sudden and flat. She always found a new man who was big in some movement or another. Supporting lettuce workers or saving seals from the business end of a Louisville Slugger.

Each time she left, I told Leonard I was through with her. And each time it was a lie. But the last time, after the Great Drunk, even I believed it.

And now she was back.

All this was going around and around in my head when she came in buck naked and put her arms around my neck and bent and kissed me on the ear. The minty clean soap smell and the aroma of sex came off her in waves. I reached up and touched her hand where it rested on my chest.

"I woke up and you were gone," she said.

"I got thirsty."

"I got horny. Come back to bed."

I stood and took her in my arms and kissed her. She was shaking from the cold. I opened my robe and stretched it around her as far as it would go and held her to me. Her hands played at my sides and rump, and finally around front where she took hold of me.

"You're pretty ruthless," I said, "treating an old man this way."

"You don't feel old, sugar."

We went back to bed, but this time she didn't let loose with the laugh I liked. She lay there when we were finished and finally eased out of bed and picked up her panties and pulled them on. I hated that. I liked the view. Covering up that downy crotch of hers with panties was as vile an act as tossing a wet bath towel over the face of the Mona Lisa.

"It's cold," I said. "Come back to bed."

"Hap, I haven't been entirely truthful with you."

"Not that you ever are. But this time, don't feel so bad. You haven't had a lot of time to lie."

She walked to the window and stood with her back to me, looking out, hugging herself. She turned slowly, her arms crossed over her breasts. "You sound pretty vindictive."

"Guess I was starting to pretend again. But you've put me back on track."

"It was always good for us, wasn't it Hap? The sex, I mean."

"For a little while, more than the sex."

She picked up my robe from where I had dropped it on the floor and put it on. She climbed into bed, crossed her legs, and sat looking at me.

"Hap, I need your help."

"I'm tapped out for money. I got maybe fifty dollars, that's it. Fifty cents in change."

"I didn't come for money."

"But you always come for something, don't you? Long as it doesn't have anything permanent to do with me."

"I don't want to argue. It's just that I need your help. I couldn't think of anyone else to ask."

"Maybe I can."

"I want you to do it, because this time you'll profit. This time will make up for all the other times."

"Nothing can make up for those times."

"This might go a long way toward it." She put her hand on my shoulder. "Hap, my love, how would you like to make an easy two hundred thousand dollars? Tax free."

3

Early next morning I left Trudy asleep and rattled my old green Dodge pickup over to Leonard's place. He had a little house off the same dirt road I lived off of, and he was only about five miles away.

I parked up close to the house, got out into the cold morning air, and tried the front door. It was locked. I got the key from its hiding place beneath the porch and let myself in.

There was a fire in the fireplace, though it had dwindled considerably, and the house smelled like coffee. I followed my nose to the kitchen and found the pot and poured a cup. I called Leonard's name, but he didn't answer.

I checked to see how his handiwork was coming. He was rebuilding his sink cabinet due to termite damage. Had precut boards stacked by the sink, a hammer and a bag of little facing nails and a bag of long nails for the wall boards. He'd been doing the work a bit at a time, and as usual with that kind of thing, his craftsmanship was excellent. Me, I couldn't put on a rubber without directions, then I might get it inside out.

I took the cup with me out the back way and walked down to the dog pens and the barn. The barn was an old-fashioned affair, once bright red and now rust-colored with big double doors and a hayloft. The pens were six long steel wire runs, and each held a spotted bird dog, and at the end of each run was a large dog house, built against heat or cold or terrific winds, and they had flap doors that closed off when the dogs went in or out. The dog in the pen closest to the barn was called Switch for some reason, and he's Leonard's favorite. Which is not to say Leonard wasn't crazy about all those big dumb bastards. He went hunting with them as often as he could, not so much to hunt, but to see those spotted beauties run.

I went by the pens, and the dogs barked and leapt. I put my fingers through the wire as I came to each run, and the dogs licked them in turn, wagged their tails and yipped.

When I got to Switch's run, I knelt down and spent more time with him. I hated to play favorites, but hell, there was something special about Switch. There was a kind of sad nobility in his eyes, like maybe he had seen some things he'd rather not have, but was the wiser for it. Which was damn silly, of course. Even a smart bird dog is a pretty dumb variety of dog. But he did have some class. He was protective of Leonard, too, and if he didn't know you and he was loose and you were standing too close to Leonard, you had to watch yourself. He'd leap at you and try to tear your face off, without so much as a bark or warning growl.

From the barn I could hear a steady thumping and knew Leonard was making that sound. He was regular about that sort of thing, even if the night before he had been up until two A. M. drinking.

I downed the rest of my coffee, finished petting Switch, stood up and leaned forward on the pen and looked out at the thick dark woods back there; they seemed to be expanding as the sunlight widened and redefined them. Leonard had a beautiful place here. The creek was maybe a little too close to the house and he'd steadily been losing his land to erosion, something his having trenches of gravel put in alongside the creek hadn't helped. For a while it was okay, but soon it broke down and the gravel started to wash away, and now sometimes in the summer we'd go stand out there on the bank and throw gravel at the water and later sit on his porch scraping it and the clay out of the treads of our shoes.

When we were really in a Huck Finn mood, we'd go down to the Robin Hood Tree, a big oak in a clearing in the woods behind Leonard's house. I don't know who all that woods belonged to, but in our minds that tree belonged to us. We'd named it that a few years back, after the big tree Robin Hood held his conferences under in Sherwood Forest. We sometimes went there to talk and enjoy the woods. Occasionally Leonard brought his rifle so he could pretend to be scouting for squirrels. But we always ended up at the Robin Hood tree, sitting with our backs against it, talking until nightfall.

My place was nice but I had to admit, I prefered Leonard's to mine. I let the look of the place soothe me while I thought about what Trudy had told me last night, and tried to figure out some way to convince Leonard to go in with me. Leonard hadn't been part of Trudy's thinking, but he was damn sure part of mine. I tried to tell myself it was because I liked Leonard and wanted to see him make some money, and though this was true, I knew too it was because I had come to depend on him so much. He had bailed me out of hell so many times, he had become my spirit guide through life.

Inside the barn the light was weak, but I could see Leonard working over the heavy bag he kept hanging from a rafter beneath the hayloft. He was stripped to the waist, wearing a pair of gray sweatpants, low-cut tennis shoes with white socks and a pair of worn bag gloves. His face and hard upper torso looked like wet chocolate, and when the light caught him right, the thick beads of sweat gave the impression of greasy boils covering his skin. He was snorting plumes of cold exhaust.

I put the coffee cup on one of the two-by-fours that helped support the unadorned wall, leaned back and watched. I guess I stood there a full five minutes before he noticed me.

"Well," he said, "you look like a man who's had sex."

"And you act like a man who hasn't. That's why you got to pound a bag, to work off frustrations."

"Tell me about it. No, don't. Just makes me feel bad." He did a combination on the bag, then smiled at me. "Unlike you, I could have all the women I want."

"Go on, talk some shit."

"Could . . . lots of them, anyway. Ain't that the shits? They want me and I don't want them. They're lined up for me, and me the way I am."

"Maybe you should try to be another way. It's bound to beat jacking off."

"Don't think it wouldn't be easier, but it's like taking up knitting or backgammon. Doesn't work for me."

"Just saying how things could be easier."

He gave the bag a flurry, then winked at me. "You could always help me out, you know. A little relief for a friend."

"I'm not that friendly."

He flurried the bag again, caught it with his forearms and smiled at me. "Got you nervous, didn't I? Tell you a truth, ole buddy. I like you, but you're not my type."

"That shatters me. I want to go right on out of here crying."

He hit the bag with two hard lefts, one high, one low. "Work the bag with me. I like to see a peckerwood sweat."

I slipped off my jacket and shirt, got the spare bag gloves off a nail, put them on, and went over to the bag. I made some slow, soft moves on it to get the muscles loose. It felt awkward at first, way it always does when you start. Then my muscles began to warm and loosen and I got my rhythm and I was circling and exploding into the bag whenever the mood struck me. Leonard was circling too, staying directly across from me, the bag between us, and no sooner would my flurry end than he would hit with a series from his side, and pretty soon we were making conga music with that old canvas bag.

When we stopped my hands ached slightly from clenching my fists, and I was beginning to breathe heavily. I took off the bag gloves, hung them up, flexed the tension out of my hands.

"You're getting soft," Leonard said, taking off his gloves. "Haven't been working out enough."

"I'm preferring my rest in my dotage."

"Want to spar some?"

"Sure."

He went over to a shelf, got down the boxing gloves and kick guards and tossed a pair of each to me. I fastened the kick guards over my tennis shoes, then pulled on the gloves. They were the kind without laces; they slid on over your hands and tightened at the wrists with elastic, so you didn't need help to get them on.

We had been using the light from the open side door, but now Leonard went over and opened the big double doors and the sun flooded in and I could see dust motes rising from the barn's dirt floor like little slow tornadoes.

Leonard put on his equipment, shuffled his feet, put up his hands and made his way toward me.

"Gonna suffer, honkie."

"Hope you know a home for invalid niggers, 'cause you're gonna need it."

"Name-calling, huh? Racial slurs."

"Call 'em like I see 'em."

"Minute from now you aren't gonna see anything."

Then we were at it.

It was like Leonard turned into oil and flowed over me. I covered up, but the oil turned hard and the hardness hit my forearms and made them weak, hit the side of my head and ribs and made sounds on my hide like the sounds Leonard and I had made on the bag.

When I got him away from me, I said, "Won't lie to you, that was nice."

"I know," he said, and came again.

I let him think he had me. I jabbed out with a weak left and when he slipped it, I kicked with my forward foot in a roundhouse motion and caught him hard enough in the bread-basket to force his breath out. I swarmed him then, hit him with a right cross above the left eye and tried to hook him with my left, but all I got was one of his forearms. He flurried me, and he was fast, but I had his timing off now, and his blows skimmed across my face and slid on my sweaty chest and didn't really hurt me. I kicked off my back leg this time and my kick caught him in the solar plexus again and drove him back and I came off the other leg and tried the same thing and glanced his side with the ball of my foot. He backed up fast, and I went after him. He turned his back on me as if to run. Instinctively I rushed in for the kill. He swiveled on his left foot and brought himself completely around to face me and his right leg arched into an outside crescent kick and the ridge of his foot caught me on the side of the head and I went down and dirt filled my nostrils.

Suckered.

Leonard bent down. "How are you, peckerwood?"

"I been worse. . . . Barn's moving, though."

"You're always impatient. I set you up." He patted me on the back. "Lay there a moment,"

"No other plans."

A few minutes passed and Leonard helped me up. The barn was still a little wobbly, but starting to shape up. He helped me get the gloves and kick guards off. I weaved over and put on my shirt and coat while Leonard did the same, then I got the coffee cup off the two-by-four and Leonard put his arm around me and walked me to the house.

Leonard put on a Patsy Cline album, turned it down low and started fixing breakfast. I took a seat at the kitchen table and dipped my head between my knees.

"You eaten?" he asked.

"No."

"Able to?"

"Yeah."

"Eggs and toast sound okay?"

"Fine."

He chuckled.

"White boys in distress," I said. "You love it."

He cracked an egg in the skillet. "You're over here for a reason, Hap. You don't get up this early on Sundays. What happened, that woman leave already?"

"Nope. But I am here for a reason. An important reason." I lifted my head. Nothing was spinning.

"How important?"

"You wouldn't have to go back to the rose fields. Least not for a long time."

He stopped unwrapping the bread and looked at me.

"How long a time?"

"Quite a few years. You might start your own business. Understand you people do well with barbecue stands, stuff like that. Whatever you want."

"Barbecue sounds like work. You know us, loose shoes, tight pussy and a warm place to shit."

"Way I heard it."

"Come on Hap, quit dicking with me. What's the deal?"

"One hundred thousand dollars for each of us."

"Shit. What we got to do, shoot someone?"

"Nope. We have to swim for it."

4

I drove Leonard to my house and parked next to Trudy's faded green Volkswagen with the Greenpeace sticker on the bumper. We went inside and found Trudy at the kitchen table drinking coffee. She was wearing one of my shirts, and it was much too large for her. That and her tousled hair made her look girlish. Less so when she crossed her legs and looked at me. "I was worried about you. I couldn't find a note."

"Didn't leave one. Thought I'd be back sooner."

She decided to notice Leonard. "Hi, Leonard."

Leonard nodded.

"What you told me last night," I said. "I want you to tell Leonard."

Her face showed me she didn't like that. "No offense, Leonard. But that was between me and Hap. He shouldn't have said anything."

"I'm dealing him in for half my share."

"There may not be a share if you keep this up, Hap."

"That's okay, too. Find some other sucker."

"You're awfully tough in the morning."

"Controls his glands better in the daytime," Leonard said. "They tend to get overactive at night."

"I don't care for the sound of your talk, Leonard," Trudy said.

"Wasn't supposed to be music," Leonard said. "Maybe you prefer a classical Negro dialect? A little foot-shuffling?"

"Can it, both of you," I said. "This is coming off worse than I thought. I want to deal Leonard in. What's it matter? It's not costing you any more, and you'll have an extra hand. Way you talk, we could use him. He's had some diving experience, for one thing. We need that. I been in the water a few times with a suit on, but that's about it."

She turned to stare out the window at the field. My mother did that when she was exasperated with me. I almost expected Trudy to threaten me with a paddling.

She turned her coffee cup around on her saucer. The light from the window was on her face and showed some of her age.

"Sometime today," Leonard said. "After a couple minutes, pouting bores me."

She looked at us. "All right, but I don't like being railroaded this way, Hap. You should have discussed it with me first. There's enough between us you could have done that."

"I didn't ask because I knew you'd say no, and I want Leonard in. It's not anything I'm trying to put over on you. He stood by me through some tough times, some of them your fault. I want to see him profit the way you say you want to see me profit. You don't want us both, no problem. Deal us out."

"It's something else to explain to Howard. He wasn't keen on me asking you in, Hap."

"I've got faith you can wrap this Howard around your big toe," Leonard said, "and I don't even know the poor sap."

"You know what's wrong with you, Leonard?" Trudy said. "You're jealous. You're in love with Hap here and you're jealous of me."

"Hap's all right," Leonard said. "He's got a nice, perky ass, but he's not my type."

"You two be friends," I said. "It's easier that way."

"I'll put a lid on it," Leonard said, "but with me and her it's business associates, not friends."

"It couldn't be any other way," Trudy said.

Leonard and I sat at the table, Leonard by the wall and me across from Trudy. She glared at Leonard, then me. "One hundred thousand is a lot less than two hundred thousand, Hap. Sure you want to do this?"

"Yep, and I want him to hear the story from you. I haven't told him anything except there's some money to be made. He hears what you got to say, he may not want in."

Trudy got up, poured another cup of coffee and came back to the table. She sipped it and started her story.

"My last husband, Howard, was involved in nuclear protests. Traveled across the country speaking against nuclear reactors, leading marches against their sites. During a protest in Utah, he was responsible for cutting a fence and getting inside a compound and damaging government property. He felt it was his responsibility as a human being—"

"No politics," Leonard said. "It affects my heart. Just the straight goods."

"All right," she said, and told it.

It was a pretty simple story. The judge made an example out of Howard. Gave him two years at my alma mater, Leavenworth, later cut it to eighteen months for good behavior. I wondered if she left Howard while he was in prison, and if he got more letters and visits than I had.

While Howard was in prison he met a man called Softboy McCall, who fancied himself a gangster. He had been in the can a while and wasn't getting out soon.

When he found out Howard was from Texas he took immediate interest in him. He was a Texan too. Waco, Texas, to be exact.

Softboy and Howard got close. Softboy told Howard what he was in for—this time anyway. He had robbed a small East Texas bank (are there any other kind?), and the day they robbed it, it was chockful of money. More money than a bank that size ought to have, even if it was a weekend and the payrolls were in.

Softboy thought it was laundered money, loot being processed through the bank by big shots. He was more certain of that later when a lesser amount than he stole was reported. Softboy claimed to have made a take just over a million.

During the robbery, there was a shootout with a guard at the bank. The police were somehow alerted, and they got there before Softboy and his two accomplices could escape, and there was more shooting. The guard and a policeman were wounded, and all three of the robbers were injured.

Still, they got in their getaway car and drove away.

Day before, the driver of the car had gone to the bottoms and found a place to hide the motorboat, and they had made for that.

Before they got to it, one of the robbers died, and when they got there, the driver went toes up. All that was left was Softboy and the money.

Softboy managed to push the car off into the water to hide it and he managed to load the money in the boat and get it going. But he didn't get far. He hit a stump or something and was thrown out.

He made it to shore, into the woods, and crawled around through the underbrush for the next three days, feverish and hallucinating. Didn't know if he was going in circles or what.

Eventually he came across a trail and followed that. Next thing he knew, he was on the highway leading to Marvel Creek. He passed out, and when he awoke he was in the Marvel Creek hospital with a policeman sitting in a chair beside his bed. Seemed some motorist had discovered him and pulled him out of the highway and called the law.

When he got better, the police tried to get him to show them where the boat had wrecked, but he couldn't.

He didn't know. He didn't even know how he and his partners had gotten the boat in the first place. He hadn't been the one who stashed it, and hadn't been along when it was stashed. After the robbery, he'd been too out of his mind with pain to notice.

The police searched the river for days, but didn't find evidence of the boat, the car, or the bodies.

Never did.

Softboy told Howard he had bad dreams about all that money underwater and the fish eating it. Said he wanted it spent, and that if Howard found it, he'd split it with him.

At this point in the story, Trudy paused and Leonard said, "Trusting sort of guy, wasn't he?"

"Suppose he thought Howard was honest enough," Trudy said. "Assumed Howard felt about him the way he felt about Howard."

"Or wanted Howard to think he felt that way." I said. "Make a guy feel wanted, he'll do things for you. Get Howard to find and coordinate the dough, and old Softboy could use it to bribe guards and prison officials. Make life a little easier in the joint. Considering his situation, it'd be a worthwhile gamble."

"Three days before they let Howard out," Trudy said, "Softboy was killed by an inmate with a knife made out of a spoon. The fight was over something silly. A dessert, I think."

"So there goes Howard's obligation to Softboy," Leonard said. "He decided to get the money, and he dealt you in, and Hap dealt me in. Well, this is all good and everything, but I see some problems here. First of all, I take it Howard's already tried to find the money. Am I right?"

Trudy nodded.

"The police have looked and Howard's looked and they've come up with nothing, so what makes anyone think we can do better?" Leonard said.

"That's where I come in," I said. "I grew up in Marvel Creek, and I know those bottoms."

"Bet a lot of folks who knew the bottoms helped the police search, and they still didn't find it," Leonard said.

"There's something else," Trudy said. "Softboy didn't tell the police about the Iron Bridge, but he told Howard."

"The Iron Bridge?" Leonard said.

"When Hap and I were married he used to talk about it some, that it was this place in the bottoms . . . How does it go, Hap?"

"It was an uncompleted bridge. Stuck out over a wide place in the water. Oil companies had started it back in the fifties before the oil ran out. All sorts of stories about that place. Lovers parked by it. There was a story about this guy went down there and hung himself off the bridge because of some girl, or some such thing. Said his ghost was still down there. That when the moon was right, you could see him hanging from the bridge. Also there's a story about this couple went down there to park, and some men came up on them, raped the girl and tied the spare tire to the guy and threw him off in the water. Lots of stories."

Trudy said, "Softboy told Howard, last thing he remembered after the wreck was lying on the bank, looking downriver and seeing the Iron Bridge."

"Thing is," I said, "the bridge isn't on the river. It's down a narrow creek that comes off of it. Don't even know if the creek's got a name. Pretty junglelike down there. Softboy could have been wounded so bad he got off the river without realizing it, but I figure they were never on it, just thought they were. They were on this creek all the time, and the only place that creek could have been wide enough and deep enough for a boat is a stretch near the Iron Bridge."

"That dough would have long dissolved and washed away by now," Leonard said. "You might find some coins, but that's about it."

"Softboy and his partners were going to carry the money downriver a ways and bury it," Trudy said. "They had another car stashed a little further on, and they thought they could get away, go back when things cooled off and recover the money. Softboy told Howard they had the money in waterproof cylinders and those were in a big aluminum cooler fastened down in the front of the boat. Chances are, the waterproof containers are still there, and so is the money."

"When was the last time you saw this bridge?" Leonard asked me.

"Eighteen, nineteen . . . maybe twenty years ago."

Leonard shook his head. "Hell, man, I've come to pick you up for work and you couldn't even find the shoes you took off the night before, let alone find something you haven't seen in twenty years."

"True . . . but my shoes didn't have a million dollars in them."

5

When we finished talking, Trudy said she was going to take a shower and lie down for a while. After being up most of the night thinking, talking, and screwing, I needed a nap too, but I refrained. I like to think it was because I had strong character. It was, of course, because I didn't want to be anywhere alone with Trudy right then. I had a hunch she would have harsh words to say about me and Leonard, and I wasn't up to it. I didn't want her to get me near a bed, either. She could really talk in bed, and if she talked long enough and moved certain parts of her body just right, I might agree to have Leonard shot at sunset.

When I heard the shower running, I got a pen and a paper and wrote Trudy a note. *Gone to Leonard's to make arrangements for leaving. Back by lunch. In case you want to come over . . .*

And I drew her a map to Leonard's house.

Me and Leonard went over to his place and he put some clothes and a paperback of *Walden* in a suitcase. He got out a thin foam rubber mattress and some blankets and rolled them up in a bundle, then got his Remington .30/06 and a box of shells out of the closet. He put the suitcase, the bedroll, the rifle, and the ammunition on the couch.

"Where's your twenty-two target pistol, Leonard?"

"Put up."

"Don't you think we might need it? Maybe you know a place that's got some bazookas and hand grenades we could buy, maybe a couple of land mines. Shit, what is all this? We're going to swim down and get some money, not shoot it."

"Comes to your ex-wife, I get paranoid."

"She's a pain in the ass, overly idealistic, but she isn't going to ambush us."

"I don't know what she might get us into. I think she leaps before she looks. And I don't know this Howard guy from nothing. He got pals, or are we the only fools in on this?"

"She said there were two others—idealists all. They're going to take their shares of the capitalist banker's money and give it to a good cause."

"No shit? What cause?"

"Save the seals, I guess. Maybe the whales. Hell, I don't know. She didn't say."

"I get any money out of this, I'm going to put it to a good cause too. Me. The seals got to fend for themselves. They don't have bills to pay."

"I hear that."

Leonard went over to the scarred fireplace mantle, got his pipe and tobacco down, and sat in the rocking chair by the fireplace. He pulled a long fireplace match out of a metal cuspidor by the hearth and put it in his lap. He packed his pipe quickly and expertly, pulled the match over the fireplace and lit it. He puffed and considered me.

"How did I let you talk me into this?"

"My perky ass had something to do with it. Christ, Leonard, perky ass?"

"I came up with that because I thought it would annoy Trudy."

"You being alive annoys her."

"Old man Lacy is gonna be needing field hands in a few days, and he'll call, and I won't be here. I'll be wasting my savings trying to find a dream in the Sabine river. Get back from this with no money and my tail between my legs, I might be out of a job permanently."

"There's always room for field hands. Look, we're out of that crap. I think we should go out and do something, even if it's wrong."

"And it is. That's stolen money."

"All this time has gone by, the insurance company is bound to have paid off, and if it's laundered, no sweat."

"How are we to know one way or the other? It might all be marked stuff, or whatever it is they do to trace money."

"We'll take our share to Mexico. We can make some deals down there. We'll have to lose a few thousand to get it changed to pesos, no questions asked, but we can do it. We can stay there awhile. The money will be worth ten times what it is here. We can buy senors for you and senoritas for me. We can get drunk on Mexican beer."

"I can't go off and leave my dogs."

"Fuck it, I'll go down there, get the money changed and mail you your half in pesos, and you can get it changed to dollars. Bring you and your goddamn dogs down there for a vacation. I'll get them some of those little Mexican dogs to date. There's some way to do business. Bank robbers do it all the time."

"You been giving this some thought. Usually Trudy comes around and you're ready to join the Peace Corps, tie yourself to a pine and save it from a chainsaw."

"Bottom's fallen out of my convictions. Trudy's got me thinking again, all right, and maybe last night she had me thinking the way she wanted, but not today."

"Like I said, Hap, it's your glands. You got more control over them in the daylight. But come sundown and you're home in bed between her legs, you might sing some different notes."

"No, she's got Howard on a string too. I can stand her coming back to me if I can fool myself for a while, but I won't sit around and let her swing from one end of the string to another."

"I didn't think it was a string she was swinging on."

"I'm going to make some jack out of this, then slide on out."

"Won't be easy. You been a bleeding heart a long time."

"This heart's bled out. Gone dry as toast. You don't think so, hide in the bushes and watch me head for Mexico."

Leonard grinned at me. "After all I've said about you being such a sap, don't know if you suit me much this way. You make me a little nervous. You being Trudy's patsy is what made you adorable. There's a kind of ignorant charm about it. Like having a big dumb pup around that hasn't quite learned to quit shitting off its papers."

"That's sweet, Leonard. I'll try to remember that."

■ ■ ■ ■

We decided to take Leonard's old blue Buick instead of my pickup. Trudy could go with us if she wanted, or go ahead in her Volkswagen. Whatever suited her. We loaded Leonard's suitcase, rifle, ammo, and bedding into the Buick's trunk, then tossed in some rope and camping supplies, just in case.

"We'll need some diving equipment," Leonard said. "Dry suits, I figure. Wet suits are probably too cold in this weather, not that a dry suit is much better. They hold pockets of air and pinch you."

"You know more about this stuff than I thought."

"Just enough to get us drowned. But I do know this. Cold as the water is right now, it'll deaden your brain. Though in your case, that may not be a new experience. I know this too: it's my goddamn savings we're using to rent this stuff."

"But you have my goodwill, Leonard."

"I been wanting that something furious."

"You rent this stuff, won't it blow our cover?"

"Hap, my good but dumb man. We aren't going to tell what we want it for. Just say we want the experience of a cold-water dive. They don't give a damn if we drown or turn to ice cubes, long as we pay down good, give them enough to buy new equipment if we lose it."

"Leonard, you're my hero. When I grow up I want to be just like you. Can I, huh, can I?"

"Need some black paint first, but that isn't gonna make you as pretty. And it would be nice if you were a lot less stupid. Come on, I need to call Calvin and see if he'll feed my dogs while I'm gone. Then I've got to cry over using all my money to finance this dumb idea. Stick close, now. Never know when I might say something wise."

6

When I awoke the next morning, I could hear the wind wolf-howling through the eaves of the house and the pines out beyond the field. At night I seldom kept the heat going, due to the price of butane, and the room was cold enough to make an Eskimo shiver.

I got up and put on my robe and padded through the morning air, blowing out puffs of whiteness as I went.

I looked out the window. The trees and the ground were iced over and there were flakes of snow mixed with sleet. Quite a rarity for East Texas. Most of the time you didn't even know it was winter; generally the winters were exaggerated falls. But this year was different. The cold had blown in hard and vicious on the very day I was supposed to start toward making some money. A wiser man would have considered it an omen.

I wanted to go back to bed, but instead I struggled to the kitchen, got matches and lit all the heaters, the one in the bedroom last. Even then, with my butt backed up to the heat, I was tempted to climb under the blankets again and snuggle close to Trudy. But it might not have been any warmer under there. She certainly hadn't been warm last night. She made love like I was paying for it and she had more customers in line, some of them important. I attempted to bring her to orgasm, but it was like trying to conquer Everest in Bermuda shorts. She wasn't having any. She wanted me to rut and feel cheap and miserable, and I did. But I have no pride and came anyway. When I finished, she rolled from beneath and turned with her back to me. I put my hand on her hip, but she didn't move or say anything. I might as well have been stroking a marble tombstone.

Suddenly I felt sorry for Howard. Like me, he didn't have a chance with a gal like Trudy. Not really. She ruled us with brains and passion and her downy triangle. It was damn demeaning is what it was.

I dressed and put on my coat and went outside and looked to see if the water in my truck's radiator was frozen. It wasn't. There had been enough antifreeze in there, and I parked it on the south side with the bumper pressed against the house and had put an old horse blanket over the hood.

I got pliers out from behind the truck seat, put the blanket under the truck from the side, crawled on top of it and worked the radiator screw loose so it would drain. This way, if I was gone for some time, I wouldn't have to worry about the cold defeating the antifreeze and blowing my ancient radiator to pieces.

I returned the blanket to the hood and found a couple rocks to put on top of it in case of high winds, then went out to the edge of my property and pried up the water cover and turned off the water valve with the pliers. I put the pliers back, went in the house and locked the windows and back door, drained the water out of the faucets, cut down the water heater, and when I heard Leonard coming, cut off the butane heaters. The air chilled immediately.

I got my gear I had packed last night and brought it into the living room and placed it by the door.

Trudy had got up and dressed during the time I was outside, and all the while I made my inside preparations, she sat on my ratty couch and looked at the wall. Didn't say a word. Didn't look to be breathing.

Leonard stepped inside, looked at Trudy, then me. "I can tell now this is gonna be fun."

"Trudy, you taking your car?" I asked.

"I'll come for it later. I'm no good driving on ice."

"Your VW hasn't got a radiator to bust," Leonard said, "but you might want to put it in my barn just the same. There's some folks in these parts might not mind stealing a car they don't know."

"What about the diving equipment?" I asked.

"In the trunk. Went in and got it yesterday, and they weren't even open. Had to talk a blue streak and wave some extra money around to get the owner out of his house and down to the shop. You owe me a hundred bucks, Hap."

"Put it on my bill."

"Man, your credit level is way topped out . . . Look, we wait a few days on this, things will be better. Ice will have blown out."

"Howard is expecting me," Trudy said. "And I have work tomorrow."

"Work?" I said.

"You know. You go to a job you hate, and they pay you money for it. You think I'm kept, Hap? Contrary to what Leonard here wants you to think, I'm not a concubine."

Over at Leonard's place, Trudy parked the Volkswagen in the barn and Leonard made up his special dog food from three different brands, poured the contents of the feed sacks in a plastic garbage can, a little bit of each, a smidgen at a time, mixing it evenly.

While he did that, Trudy walked out to the dog pens and I followed. I felt like I ought to say something, but didn't know what. She had a way of making me feel like a jerk when I hadn't done anything. We both stood by the dog pens and waited on Leonard. We were at the end opposite Switch's run, and Trudy had her fingers poked through the wire and was scratching the nose of a dog named Cal, cooing sweet things to him. The dog was eating it up. I was eating it up secondhand. She sounded very sexy making those tender little sounds, and bless my little heart, I wanted to make love to her so bad right then I thought I'd cry.

Leonard came out of the barn and started in our direction. On his way over, he stopped, knelt down to reach his fingers through the wire of Switch's run so the dog could lick his fingers. "Get in your doghouse, boy. You gonna freeze your nuts off."

Switch was acting like a pup, wagging his tail so hard his entire body shook. I walked down to them, and forgot Trudy. She came after me and suddenly knelt between me and Leonard and put her hand to pet Switch the way she had Cal.

Switch, quick and silent as an arrow, leapt for her extended fingers. Leonard snatched her hand back and Switch's muzzle went against the wire. He grabbed it with his teeth, pulled, let go with a snap. Foam flecked out of his mouth and splashed on the knee of my jeans. Trudy hadn't even had time to flinch.

Leonard let go of her hand, and Trudy stepped back. "Jesus! What's in him?"

"Protective," Leonard said. "He doesn't like anyone near me he doesn't know. That dog and men like me, probably the only males you can't twist the way you want."

"You think it's funny, don't you, Leonard?" Trudy said.

"He got your fingers, I wouldn't. Since he didn't, yeah, I think it's funny."

"You can have your old dog. I hope he freezes to death."

"Good thing I don't think you mean that, lady."

Trudy walked away quickly.

"Glad you don't like women," I said, "because you don't exactly have a way with them."

"I like women fine, just not to fuck. And I don't like that woman to do anything with. You think the dogs are gonna be cold?"

"Hell yeah. But the way you've got their houses fixed up, they'll be all right. Warmer than we're going to be. Calvin comes to feed them, sees they're uncomfortable, he'll do something about it."

"Yeah . . . guess so."

Then we were all in the Buick, easing along with Leonard at the wheel, me in the front, leaning on the door as if contemplating a leap, and Trudy dead center of the backseat with arms and legs crossed tight as the coils of the Gordian knot.

The car leaked carbon monoxide through a hole in the floorboard and we were all a little dizzy from it. The wipers beat at the snow and ice and the near-bald tires whistled a tentative funeral march. We made it slow and easy, without much talk, into Marvel Creek about half-past noon.

7

The town really started before the city limits. There was a line of beer joints on either side of the highway, ramshackle fire hazards with neon pretzels on their roofs and above their doorways.

Among them were two places I well remembered: The Roundup Club and The Sweet White Lilly.

Next came the long, wide river bridge and the city limits sign that read POP. 5606. Then we were on Main Street, coasting past closed businesses with boarded windows and bolted doors, service stations with oil spotted drives and greasy-capped men with their hands on gas nozzles or leaky tires.

As we went deeper into town, it got better. Open stores and more people. But the place still looked sad. Not that it had been any budding metropolis when I lived there.

Trudy had us turn on a brick street slick as vaseline, and we went past the bank, around a curve and past what had been a Piggly Wiggly but was now called Food Mart. I used to buy Cokes and peanut patties there, hang out with the boys and lie about all the fights I'd been in and all the tail I'd banged.

We glided past car lots and the empty spot where the Dairy Queen had stood and old Bob used to make us chocolate shakes with more water than milk in them. On down the highway we went, onto a blacktop and back into the pines, and finally down a soggy clay road that ended at a small house that was mostly weathered gray with strips of paint peeling down its sides like melted candle wax. The front porch leaned starboard and the smoking, crumbling chimney was held upright by the slanting support of ten feet of warped six-by-six. Pine sap corrosion had turned the mouth of the chimney dark as the devil's shadow.

Parked off to the right on the dead grass were a red, dented Dodge mini-van and a jaundice-yellow Volvo with a sheet of cardboard in place of the left front window. Two more letters on the end and the writing on the cardboard would have read MONTGOMERY WARD.

Leonard killed the engine, looked at me, and said, "And I thought *we* lived like trash."

Trudy got out of the car without saying anything and we stayed where we were. Before she was all the way up the porch steps, the door opened and a big, handsome blond guy with a slight gut, wearing jeans, a gray sweat suit, and old hightop white tennis shoes came out. He took Trudy in his arms and kissed her in a more than cordial fashion.

"Flexible, ain't she." Leonard said. "And you know, bubba, he's prettier than you are."

The guy who had to be Howard looked at us. He said something to Trudy and then came out to the car. We got out before they could get there and leaned on the hood and tried to look thuggy.

"This is Howard," Trudy said.

"You must be Hap," Howard said. "I've heard a lot about you."

We shook hands.

"This is Leonard," Trudy said.

It was obvious from the expression on Howard's face he was trying to picture Leonard's role in all this. "So, you gave Trudy and Hap a ride up. You ought to stay for dinner before you go back. I'm going to fix my famous spaghetti dinner."

"He's in on it," I said.

"Ah," said Howard, and looked at Trudy.

She wouldn't let him catch her eye. "He's a good swimmer," she said. "Hap wouldn't come without him. It's like they're married or something."

"Just engaged, " Leonard said. "We're still picking china."

Howard had gone mildly red-faced with irritation. "So, you swim, huh?"

"Like a goddamn eel," Leonard said.

Howard nodded, tried to keep it pleasant. "Where's your car, Trudy?"

"Leonard's. I didn't want to drive on ice."

"I see," Howard said. "What say we go in? I'm freezing."

"Go ahead," Leonard said. "I'm gonna smoke a pipeful first. Hap's gonna keep me company."

"All right," Howard said, and put his arm around Trudy as they started for the house. Howard seemed to be holding her shoulders rather tight.

They went inside and Leonard got his pipe and fixings out of his coat pocket, packed the pipe, and lit it.

"I don't know about you, Hap, but I liked him. He's sweet. Warmed to me right off, don't you think?"

"I think you talk too much."

"And I could see he warmed to you too, and you to him. You both got, I don't know, a kind of glow on your faces when you first saw one another. Guess spreading the same gal does that to you."

We leaned on the hood for about five more minutes, then Leonard tapped out his tobacco and put his foot on it. "Well," he said, "what say we go on up to the house and meet the rest of the gang? Got a feeling we're gonna love them as much as we do Howard."

8

The house was sticky-warm and the air wore the smell of incense like a coat, and beneath the coat was some kind of stink.

The incense came from the upraised trunk of a small brown ceramic elephant sitting in the middle of a water-ringed coffee table. My delicate nose determined that the underlying stink most likely came from the kitchen garbage. The heat came from a big butane heater with busted grates, and from a small fireplace that needed shoveling out.

The walls were covered with faded newspaper, and the paper was ripped and peeling, and where it was completely gone you could see pocks in the wood and occasional holes stuffed with thick wads of toilet tissue.

There was a couch covered in what was left of a flowered pattern, and a big green armchair with the cloth on its arms worn down to the wood and cotton dangling out of the cushions like some strange animal that had got its guts knocked out by a speeding car.

There were also a couple of folding metal chairs with their seats polished silver by hordes of shifting asses.

"All right," Leonard said. "Where's everybody?"

As if in answer, Howard came through a door. Before he closed it, I saw behind him a kitchen with a greasy cookstove, a bullet shaped refrigerator and smoky-yellow walls that were once white.

I was right about the garbage too. With the kitchen door open the smell came into the room like a bully and started pushing the incense around. Howard closed the door, stopped in the center of the living-room and stood there looking nervous and angry, though he was trying not to let it show, and thought he was good at it. He was all dry smiles and no hand gestures—he had his hands pushed down in his pockets to keep from it, but there was tension in them and they fluttered in his pants like frightened animals trapped in sacks.

"Trudy went to tell the others," he said. "They'll want to meet you."

"Bet they aren't as excited about it as we are," Leonard said.

The door to the hallway opened and saved Howard from having to respond to that. Trudy came into the room, along with some cooler air and a fat, doughy man with a shaggy haircut that didn't go with his receding hairline. He wore a tie-dyed T-shirt, faded jeans with ripped-out knees, and low-cut work shoes with thick white socks. Except for the haircut and clothes, he was a pretty nondescript guy. He had colorless eyes, shit-brown hair and smooth features.

But the only thing regular about the man who followed him were the clothes he wore: a black T-shirt with pocket, blue jeans and running shoes.

The right side of his face was red and angry, obviously burn-scarred. He had a lump like a melted candle for a nose. His lips were two thin lines of purple leather. His left ear was missing and there was a knob of wart-like flesh where it had been. He was bald except for a tuft of hair over his right ear, and that ear seemed big enough and flared enough to pick up Radio Free Europe. At some point his scalp had been torn off and resewn, and a poor job had been done of it. The skin on the back of his head pouched up like a wrinkled pup tent.

Trudy said to me, "I've explained to them that you and Leonard are with us."

"Except I'm not giving my share to any whales or such," Leonard said.

Trudy didn't bite. She was learning to ignore Leonard. Things went better that way. She gestured to the doughy man, said, "This is Chub."

Chub came forward, put his hand out and I took it and we shook. "Real name is Charles," he said, "Everyone calls me Chub because I'm a little pudgy."

I didn't know what to say to that, so I smiled like a jackass and Chub went to Leonard and shook his hand, said, "Trudy just told us about her hesitation in letting you in on our plans here, and I want to assure you it had nothing to do with you being black. That isn't our way. We make our decisions on a one-to-one basis."

Leonard said, "You keep your dialogue on a three-by-five card?"

Chub grinned. "I accept that. I learned years ago, if you express what you think and feel, you're better off than if you don't."

"Chub's had analysis," the burned man said, "and he never lets us forget it."

"It's done me a world of good," Chub said. "There was a time when being the fat kid, the one who got chosen last in football, the one who didn't get the pretty girls or get asked to go riding around with the popular boys, was painful and important. It carried over into being an adult. But analysis has allowed me to move beyond that and I can accept who I am."

"Yeah, but I don't think I can," Leonard said.

"That's right," Chub said. "Express yourself. I'm not offended."

"Before he expresses himself in a way you don't want, Chub," the burned man said, "let me introduce myself. I'm Paco."

"Paco what?" Leonard said.

"Just Paco."

Paco didn't come forward to shake hands, and we didn't go to him. I stood there feeling foolish. Leonard probably felt disgusted, and with good reason. What had seemed like a good idea yesterday now seemed childish and pathetic. Reality had taken hold and I felt like a little boy who had been playing at adventurer but had just been told by mother to put my toys away and come in to supper.

We stood that way a long time. Leonard said, "Isn't anyone going to ask me my sign?"

Chub said, "I sense a lot of hostility in you, Leonard. I'd like to know you better, have you think of me as a friend, someone you can talk to. Being able to talk things out can really let off pressure."

"Chub," Leonard said, "that analysis shit might be all right for an airhead like you, but you come at me again with that, I'm gonna let off that pressure you're worried about."

Chub started to open his mouth, then mulled it over. His lips twitched, like the words were living things trying to push out. But he held them. Leonard looked like a man who just might let off pressure.

I felt sorry for poor Chub on one hand, but on the other he sort of asked for what he got. Kind of wore a perpetual KICK ME sign around his neck and on his ass.

"We're not getting off to the best start," Howard said. "There's no need for threats."

"He wants to talk like people talk, okay," Leonard said, "but he wants to play analyst, he can talk that trash to himself."

"We're going to work together," Howard said, "we got to coexist."

"True," Paco said, "but could be a solid punch in the teeth would do Chub some good. I'm tired of him myself." He looked over at Chub. "One word about my physical scars being a manifestation of my internal condition, or some dumb thing like that, and I'm going to promise you something similar to what Leonard promised."

Chub put his hands in his pockets and smiled to let us know he could take whatever was dished out. He was okay, you were okay.

"Violence isn't the way here," Howard said. "Let's sit down and get something to drink or smoke and talk business. We'll eat in a while."

"That sounds right enough," Leonard said.

"Trudy," Howard said, "will you help me bring in some drinks?" Then to us, "Selection's limited. Coke, beer, some Dickle whisky. We got a little grass, anyone wants it."

Chub didn't want anything. I went for beer. Paco and Leonard took the Dickle.

Trudy caught my eye and gave me a look that pinned my skull to the wall. Gee, what did I do? Leonard was the bigmouth. I thought I'd been pretty sweet, all things considered.

I tried smiling at her, but she wasn't going for that. She

turned her back, and she and Howard went into the kitchen and closed the door.

Paco went over to Leonard, grinned and said, "By the way, big fella, what *is* your sign?"

"The Asshole," Leonard said.

"I'll buy that," Paco said.

Chub smiled. He smiled big. He liked himself. He and the world were one with one another. Except he was smiling so tight the muscles in his cheeks were quivering.

In the kitchen I could hear Howard murmuring, and though I couldn't understand what he was saying, I could tell from the tone of his voice that Leonard and I had already worn out our welcome, or Leonard had worn it out for both of us. Not that it mattered. Now that we were dealt in, they had to let us stay. Thing was, I wasn't sure there was anything to stay for.

That feeling of foolishness washed over me again, big time.

9

After a bit, Trudy and Howard came back with our drinks, and I sat on the couch with them. Leonard got the gutted chair, and Paco and Chub pulled the folding chairs up close. Howard sipped a beer and went through the stuff Trudy had told us about the money most likely being laundered. Then he started waving his hands around and working his best facial expressions; threw in a few cents about how the spirit of the sixties need not die; how the money we were going to get could be used to push the ideals of that time forward; said the survivors of that noble era need not fall by the wayside; that unlike the dinosaur our generation had been compared to, we were not in fact extinct or even on the endangered species list, we were merely hibernating like a bear, and now was the time to awake to a new and productive spring.

Although Howard pretended to be talking to both me and Leonard, it was pretty clear it was me he was trying to interest. Trudy had told him about my past, about my involvement in "the movement," and he thought he might jump start my old battery if he could find the right words.

He couldn't.

I was curious about what they had in mind, but felt it would be a mistake to go the next step and ask. I'd open a whole new can of germs that way. Once they knew I was interested they'd try to work their virus into my bloodstream and take over, and I couldn't see any reason to go through the process.

From the way Trudy looked at me, I think she was both surprised at me and disgusted with me. I don't know if it was my lack of interest in their cause, whatever it was, or the realization she was losing control over me.

During Howard's dissertation on the sixties and what it meant to him and should mean to all of us, Chub threw in a few "right ons," but for the most part was mercifully silent. Paco yawned a lot, and Trudy tried to stare me into submission. I attempted to look pleasant but a little dense, like a dog listening to a talk on nuclear physics.

When Howard was on his third run of rephrasing what he'd already said, hoping to sneak up on my blind side, Leonard said, "Since I don't see we're talking much business, pardon me, will you? Because like the bear coming out of hibernation and feeling the first intestinal stirrings of spring, I've got to take me a big, greasy shit. When y'all get to the folk songs part, maybe I'll come back. I'm good on 'I Got A Hammer.'"

"Wrong era," I said. "We're talking Beatles and Doors here."

"I never can fit in," Leonard said, "and I try so goddamn hard."

He went in search of the bathroom.

"Your friend doesn't seem to like us much," Howard said.

"No, he doesn't," I said. "He wasn't involved in any movement during the sixties except moving out of the way of bullets, trying not to get his ass shot off in Vietnam."

Howard nodded like that explained some things. "He knows about guns, I presume?"

"Yeah, got a medal or two in Vietnam. But on the negative side he's a little weak on the social graces and Bob Dylan lyrics, and I've caught him in a few mistakes when we're discussing the ballet and the history of Marxism."

"I don't get the impression you're all that interested in reviving the spirit of the sixties, either," Howard said.

"Can't imagine why you thought I might be. Well, I can imagine, but whatever Trudy's told you about me, that's in the past. This sixties talk is embarrassing. You sound like a first-year college guy who's just gotten away from mom and dad and discovered weed and liberal politics."

"The sixties were a positive time, a good time," Howard said.

"Some of it was. Some of it wasn't. But that was the sixties. I'm happily selfish now. I'm in this for the money alone. Besides, sounds to me like you're trying to justify theft with sixties rhetoric, and you're too goddamn secretive for my taste. You sound like more illegal stuff than I've agreed to, and I don't want to hear about it. I'm not going to prison for some idealistic rush. This idealism crap has got me nowhere but tired and broke and cut to the bone. Money I can spend, and might get away with it.

"I can take it and go someplace warm with cheap whisky and loose women." I looked at Trudy. "Women that want nothing more than hot, sticky sex down Mexico way or on some tropical island where you can run around with your ass hanging out and your dick slapping your thigh, and nobody asks you anything but mind your own business. You people fight the good fight, whatever it is, because you're going to have to do it without us."

Paco grinned, got out a cigarette pack, lipped a smoke and lit it with a cheap lighter.

"Don't make us breathe your bad air," Howard said.

"Screw you," Paco said. He blew smoke across the room.

Normally I'd be on Howard's side, but I enjoyed seeing him irritated. I almost asked Paco for a cigarette.

Howard sighed, looked at Trudy sadly; he was a smart, hip guy dealing with a bunch of nincompoops. What could he do?

"Anytime change is encouraged," Chub said, "there's always someone who argues for the status quo, or decides to run off and take it easy, concludes that the best and simplest way—"

Paco reached over and slapped Chub on top of the head with his fingers.

"Damn you," Chub said. "That was childish, Paco. You're frustrated about something, you should discuss it, not resort to—"

Paco slapped Chub again, this time with the palm of his hand, said, "Shut up, will you, Chub?"

"Who's side you on, Paco?" Howard asked.

"Yeah," Chub said, rubbing his head.

"I'm not choosing up," Paco said. "I'm tired of Chub's bullshit is all. He keeps talking like he's done some things. Hell, leave Hap alone. He isn't interested. Let him and Leonard do their job, then let's do what we're gonna do. They couldn't care less. If they want it that way, lets leave it that way. You guys are starting to sound like evangelists, and I hate those fuckers."

"Amen." It was Leonard back from the bathroom.

"You look refreshed," I said. "Hope you struck some matches."

"About four. It was a championship shit."

"I can see this isn't going anywhere," Chub said. "So I think I'll withdraw until we're willing to converse sensibly."

"Telling it like we see it," Leonard said. "Isn't that what you like, Chubby?"

"I don't need this," Chub said. He got up and went through the hallway door.

"I hate it when he leaves the room," Leonard said. "He makes things so damn bright when he's around. But since he's gone, I'm going outside to smoke."

"Thanks for not cluttering up the air," Howard said, and he looked at Paco.

Paco put a smile on his ugly face and kept smoking.

Leonard said, "It's not your air I'm worried about. It's mine. This place has a rot smell under all that fucking incense. Smelled enough of that in Vietnam. The rot and the incense."

Leonard went outside.

"Think I'll join him," Paco said, and he got up and went out and closed the door.

"Me too," I said, and got up and started after Paco.

"Hap," Trudy said. "We got to talk."

God had spoken. "Do we?" I said.

"I told you you shouldn't have done this," Howard said to Trudy.

"You don't know everything," Trudy said and stood up.

"I know this," Howard said. "I know this isn't a good idea at all. You're thinking maybe with some other part of your body."

"That's rich, coming from you," Trudy said. "I've seen how you think."

"How you make me think."

"Children," I said. "Let's not fight."

Howard stood up, held his beer in my direction. "I got something to say to you, big shot."

"Say it, then," I said, "while I'm used to the drone of your voice. I'd rather not get acclimated again."

"You think you can come in here and run things," he said, "be a goddamn comedian. But you're wrong."

"I'm not trying to run anything. I just don't want to be ran."

"We got some scruples here. Idealism may strike you as dumb, or sissy, or childish, or nostalgic, but there's more to it than that. There's more to us than that."

"I'm sure history will be kind to you," I said. "Howard gave his stolen money to the whales. He was a good guy. Hap gave his to wine and heat and women. He was a a bad guy. Leonard bought all the Hank Williams originals he could find. He was a bad guy."

"What's with the whales?" Howard said. "No one's said a thing about the whales."

"Shut up," Trudy said. "You're drunk."

"Only had a beer," he said.

"The smell of rubbing alcohol makes you silly," she said.

"Look, Howard," I said, "I'm not trying to cause any trouble here. You think maybe I'm trying to take Trudy—"

"She's her own person," Howard said.

"Yeah, but you don't like the fact that I've been fucking her again, do you?"

"Hap," Trudy said. "Don't."

"You know I have," I said. "You think she came over to my place and merely talked some business? We banged each other till our eyes bugged out."

"Like Howard said, Hap, he doesn't own me. And neither do you."

"And I'm damn proud of it," I said.

What Howard thought he knew, he was now certain he knew. In theory it was okay, but in actuality it got under his skin like a chigger.

"It doesn't matter," Howard said, but his voice lacked conviction. "She's a grown woman. I've got no strings on her."

"But she's got them on you," I said. "And I should know. They used to go all the way through me and fasten to the bones. I got maybe a few still tied in me. Enough that I'm acting horsey here when I shouldn't, and it's making you do the same."

"I'm saying you're not coming in here and changing what we believe, what we're going to do. That's all. I'm not saying anything about me and Trudy or you and Trudy."

"I think you're saying plenty about just that. You open your mouth and your heart and dick talk over you. Like I said, I'm one to know."

"You don't know anything," Howard said. "You and that other guy, you think you know all there is to know, but you don't know a thing."

"Let's leave it," I said. "I don't want to hear any more. So it isn't the whales. Do what you got to do for people and animals and nuclear disarmament, and give my regards to the boys in Leavenworth."

"To hell with you, pilgrim," Howard said. He moved around the coffee table, staggered slightly. That bit of alcohol really had got to him. Or maybe it was the capper to some he drank earlier. Had I been in his place, knowing Trudy was supposed to be with me but was off with one of her ex-husbands for a few days, I'd have been drinking too. At one point I had.

He came around the coffee table and put his hand out and pushed me hard in the chest, but made the mistake of not pulling back fast enough, and I put my hand over the back of his, trapped it to my chest and bent forward. It sent Howard to his knees. It was a playground trick, but heck, he started it.

"Stop it, Hap," Trudy said. "Let him go."

I let him go. Trudy bent down and put an arm around him and tried to hoist him up. He shrugged her off, got up on his own.

He pointed a finger at me, but he wasn't standing as close as before. "Try that when I haven't been drinking."

"Okay," I said.

"Hell, listen to me," he said. "I'm playing your macho game now. I'm not getting pulled into this. I'm gonna lie down. I've had all this foolishness I want."

Without wobbling too much, he went through the hallway door and out of sight. Maybe he and Chub had their own special place to sulk back there. Some old sixties records to play.

"Happy?" Trudy said.

"Semi."

1 0

I awoke to the sound of a bird and the embrace of the cold. The voice of the bird was pathetic, and the cold was criminal.

I was on the back porch of the little house, and it had once been screened in, and in a sense still was, but to make it a kind of room, cardboard had been tacked all around on the screen in a couple of layers. It might have worked okay summers, but winters, especially this winter, it wasn't much.

I wondered whose idea it was to fix the porch this way. The landlord or the renters? I voted on the renters. A landlord who'd let people live in this shit box didn't strike me as the type to bother with even cardboard siding.

Originally Leonard and I had been in the kitchen, sleeping on the floor. The cookstove, with the oven door open, heated up the small room perfectly. But I awoke in the middle of the night bathed in sweat, finding it hard to breathe. I opened the door that lead out to the back porch, and that helped some, but the air in the kitchen was still poisonous with butane. I toed Leonard awake and told him I was going out on the porch, and if he didn't want to spend tomorrow in Marvel Creek Funeral Home, he might want to do the same.

Now I was lying under some ice-crusted blankets, inside an old sleeping bag. The bag was on top of some broken down cardboard boxes (probably the remains of the interior decorating scheme) and the seams on the cardboard had worked through the bag and into my back. I was still in my clothes. My socks felt damp from yesterday's sweat. My body felt stiff as wire.

I rolled over, and sitting in the kitchen doorway with a blanket over his shoulders, shivering, looking at me in what can only be called an unpleasant manner, was Leonard. His breath was snorting out of his mouth and nostrils in white puffs and his eyes were narrow.

He said, "I've let you talk me into some shit before, Hap, but this one is the king of all the dumb things. These fuckers are seriously balled up. Ought to have my ass kicked, and be proud of it."

"Good morning."

"Chub is really in orbit, and Howard is so full of what Trudy's filled him with, he doesn't know if he needs to shit or throw up."

"Don't you have something unpleasant to say about Paco? You wouldn't want to leave anybody out."

"He confuses me. He doesn't seem like part of this. He's got his feet on the ground."

"You're just sweet on him because he went out on the porch and had a smoke with you."

"Yeah, that's it."

"They're kind of silly, Leonard, but they've got good intentions. Without people like these sillies, blacks would still be drinking at water fountains that said colored and they'd be going around back of a restaurant to get their food through a little slot."

"Now you're talking like the fat guy."

"He's a clown, but his heart's in the right place."

"Tell me about women's rights now. Toss in something about how the gays used to be more oppressed before people like these, people like you, came along. Tell me how you people ended the war."

"All true."

"Then why the hell didn't you go for what they wanted you to go for yesterday? They were fishing with every kind of bait they had."

"I guess it's their posture. That holier than thou attitude that smacks more of a performance than anything else."

"I thought you said it was heartfelt."

I hate being caught in a contradiction. "Have you ever thought about fucking yourself, Leonard?"

"Constantly. Want to have a relationship with a good man, figure I'd be prime pick. But my dick's about a half-inch too short to get the job done. I like to feel it all the way up in my liver."

"You through jacking with me now?"

"Almost. All I got to say is you can't be a professional bleeding heart. Yeah, things are better for blacks and women and gays, but it was the blacks and women and gays that did it, not fuck-ups like this bunch. Whites and straights came along to give help, all right, after the blacks said 'enough' and got their heads busted, and it's the same for the gays and the women. The whites and straights, they control things, and they could have changed it anytime."

"Not all us whites and straights are in a position of power, or haven't you noticed?"

"Let's save this for next time we're on *Meet The Nation* or something."

"Gladly. I'm too cold to argue, and if I got up from here to kick your ass my foot would break off."

"Or I'd break it off for you. Now that's settled, let's get out of here before the World Savers get up."

Leonard looked at his watch. "It's six o'clock and I'm hungry. Paco said there's a pretty good place for breakfast in town."

"Maybe they got something here we could fix."

"Nothing in the fridge but a bag of uncooked spaghetti and three beers. Cabinets are mostly empty, except for some roaches."

We left without disturbing anyone, went out to Leonard's car, and it cranked after a scary moment of the starter Bendix clicking. As we drove away, I thought of Trudy and Howard in bed together and felt like Howard must have felt when she was with me.

Depressed.

I thought of them lying there, her waking up, giving herself to him before she got cleaned up and went off to work (wherever she worked) and he went to his job (if he had one). Then I imagined them coming home from a hard day, planning to steal money that was already stolen to use for some noble cause. Ozzie and Harriet of the sixties set.

I liked it. It was sweet. They were a great couple with high ideals.

I hoped it was so cold back there her vagina was frozen shut. Sue me. I've got a juvenile streak.

11

We drove in and found a little café called Bill's Kettle, the place Paco recommended. It hadn't been there when I was growing up. Back then that spot had been a magazine and cigar store. The lady who ran it used to let me read comics off the rack and not buy them. I was the only one she let do that.

The building the café was in, though it had to be considerably younger than the one the magazine store had occupied, looked much older. It appeared to be held up with nothing more than the smoke and grease from the kitchen. The huge plate glass was so grimy you could hardly see movement behind it. Someone had made an attempt to wipe it clean on the outside but hadn't bothered rinsing the soap; it looked like the end result of a Halloween prank.

The inside looked no better. The floors were scuffed and dirty and tables had been poorly wiped. There were two men at one table eating. They eyed us and nodded as we came in. In the back a young man sat staring into space, sipping coffee. There was a fat blond woman in thinning green stretch pants at the counter. She gave us a quick glance and went back to her coffee and cigarette, said something to the thin, oily-headed man behind the counter. He managed a laugh, like a leukemia patient trying to be cheery.

We sat and kept our arms off the table. The fat blond woman

got down off the stool and came over with menus. Pretty sneaky, the help blending in with the clientele that way.

We ordered, and about the time our meal arrived, Paco came in. He had on faded khakis and a blue baseball cap today. The cap hid some of the ugliness of his head. No one stared; they all worked at not doing that, and you could tell.

He saw us, smiled, and the smile was nice; the only part of him that wasn't ruined.

He came over and Leonard made room and Paco sat down beside him. We went through the casual greeting bullshit you go through, and the waitress shrugged off the stool and came over with her cigarette in her mouth and asked around it for Paco's order, then went away.

"She didn't even bother with a menu," Leonard said.

"I always get the same thing," Paco said. "Pancakes. Her asking me is simply a ritual."

Surprise. The food was great. I was wiping up the last of my eggs with a piece of toast when Paco smiled at me and said, "Place looks like a toilet, but what comes out of the kitchen could pass for ambrosia. They got someone back there knows what cooking is all about."

When Paco's order came and he finished eating, I said, "How do you live, you and the guys? Trudy the only one working?"

"I don't get too many indoor jobs with this face," Paco said. "Nobody in a store wants to look at me all day. I do some jobs here and there. Move across country doing different things, farm and yard work mostly. Sometimes things that aren't legal or aren't quite legal. Right now, you could say I'm between jobs.

"Trudy works at the Dairy Palace east of town. She doles out hamburgers. I'll tell you now. Don't eat there. The food's for shit.

"Howard's got a job at a gas station. Pumps gas, changes tires, fixes flats, runs the wrecker service. He's getting in good with the owner so he can get use of the wrecker. Told the guy that way his wife—Trudy's going as his wife—won't have to pick him up. He thinks they're gonna let him have the wrecker soon and we can use it to pull the boat out some afternoon."

"If there is a boat," Leonard said.

"I don't let myself think any other way," Paco said. "There's a boat."

"You got Trudy's kind of dedication," I said.

"I don't know she's so dedicated," Paco said. "She wants to be, but I don't know she is. I don't know her like Howard knows her, or maybe you know her, but I know her type. I've heard her talk about you two, and I've heard Howard talk, and I see how burned out you are, Hap, and I got to draw some conclusions. I think she's a quitter. She likes to get all the sticks and tinder for the fire, likes to light it, but doesn't want to be there when it starts to smoke too much and get too hot. By then, she's out of there, gathering new sticks, starting new fires, then she's away from that one before it gets going good. Leaves someone else to mind the blaze, lets them take the heat and smoke and get all burned up. She's got a knack for picking guys who'll martyr for her, ones who think she's gonna come back and burn up with them."

"I been trying to tell this clown that for years," Leonard said. "I know a goddamn succubus when I see one."

"What about you, Paco?" I asked. "What's your story? You just dedicated to their cause, or what?"

"Me, I'm not dedicated at all. Except to myself. I'm just looking to score as big as I can."

"I hear that," Leonard said. "But what are you doing with these bozos?"

"I'm a bozo too. Or have been. I'm just not dedicated anymore. I'm like a big truck with momentum and no brakes, the gearshift knob off in my hand, going downhill on a narrow grade. I want to stop but can't. I got to ride things out. Either I go over the side or make it to the bottom of the grade and coast out smooth and easy, hope I don't wreck."

"Chub?" I asked.

"He was born with money. He hung around with ill-contents. It gave him a club. He's still eighteen or twenty in his head. Never really gets up against the hub, just likes to think he does. Always been a weekend rebel, but he's gone and got married to getting this money. He wants to use it to fight some injustice. Anyway, folks back home in Houston disowned him, but not before they gave him a bundle they thought he'd use on becoming a doctor. Over the years, he's spent most of it on good causes, got some in the bank here to live on. He's got degrees aplenty. Knows medicine, even though he never became a doctor. Wouldn't go the final business because he thought that was becoming part of the establishment. He's got idealism like nerds got religion or *Star Trek*."

"I still don't have you figured in all this," I said.

"Maybe when I see that money I won't do what they think. But I don't see any cause to rock the boat until we got the boat. We work together, we might can bring that money up. They think I got other plans, they might fade on me. It's not like I can go to the police and complain I been welched on. Besides, if I could, I wouldn't. I got some problems there already."

"Suppose you're going to tell us about it?" Leonard said.

"We're gonna break the law together, so why not?" Paco got out a cigarette and lighter and lit up. He looked around. The fat blond waitress was gone from the counter—somewhere in the back, most likely. The fella behind the cash register was leaning on it, looking out that grimy glass. We were the only customers left in the place.

Paco said, "I got a record. It's the sixties' fault. Well, my fault and the sixties with it, but it's no fun blaming yourself even if you think you're guilty. So I'm gonna say it's the sixties fault and you can know better if you want.

"But when it was '68 I graduated and went off to the University of Texas, and things were heated up good, what with the war and all. Back then I had a face. I wasn't a Greek god or nothing, but I wasn't so bad. Now I scare crows at a hundred yards. But the face was all right, and I guess I was all right too. Full of lies about life and all, like we all are then. But I started figuring out some things. Come to the conclusion what we been told about things, about life, is just talk. You act a certain way to gain a certain thing, and that's all there is to it. I know that now, but then, I was full of love and peace and end the war, civil rights and women's rights. Thought I could make everyone look at these things and see that's the way it ought to be, that it would hit them like a thunderbolt from Zeus.

"I got a feeling you know what I'm saying, Hap, I know a disfranchised sixties guy when I see one."

"You pegged him right," Leonard said.

"Silence in the gallery," I said.

"So, anyway, I'm off to college, and I'm Mr. Big Shot. I'm gonna do some things. I know how the world works and I'm gonna rip off the lid and let everyone look inside and see the gears, and once they do, it's all gonna go smooth. We'll put a little oil in there, but once the machinery of a thing is understood, there goes the mystery. Everyone can live together and love one another, no sweat.

"But when I finally got the lid off, looked down there, I saw the machinery was a lot more complex than I originally thought. You couldn't glance at it and see how it worked. I had to go down in the machine and study it, become a mechanic. Change some things around so it was simple. I figured I could do that. Figured when I came up out of the machine, it would be smooth and well oiled and would run the way it was supposed to. Without prejudice and wars and sexism. People would be kind to animals, loan their tools, and locks would come off doors."

I nodded. "Peace, brother."

"You got it. So I decided to team up with these other mechanics. People who had the right ideas, you know, wanted to get down in that machinery with me, do some work. This machinery analogy was theirs, and they started calling themselves the Mechanics. You don't hear much about them some reason or another, but they were active as ants."

"I heard of them," I said. "Started out getting people to register to vote. Pushing the ideas of a democracy, then they splintered. The ones that continued to call themselves the Mechanics were kind of like the radical branch that split off from the Students for a Democratic Society and called themselves the Weathermen."

"You got it. The splinters all died out pretty quick without their original leader. He was a charismic kind of guy. Had come into the group as one of the Indians, but in no time was chief. A few of the Indians split, tried to form their own tribes, but the diehards stayed with him. And it took him to hold things together, keep the Mechanics on track.

"So the Mechanics got their monkey wrenches and went to work. Said to hell with this democratic society shit, the answers are in the street. You got to wreck some things to get them built up new and different. We went underground. Got guns, started hitting anyplace we thought didn't jive with human rights or supported the war in Vietnam. There were lots of targets. We bombed a few ROTC buildings throughout the state. Moved on to other states. Traveled all over and didn't get caught. We were a different kind of criminal than the FBI had dealt with before. Smart people with a smart leader. We had a cause, and there's no one more dangerous than the zealot, and we were that in spades."

"How many of you were there?" Leonard asked.

"Twelve at first. Took in a few more here and there off college campuses. Did some sneaky recruiting. We had been students, so we knew where to go to talk to the right people—people with a similar political mind. We hooked them in, fed them radicalism like pudding. The leader of the Mechanics was especially good at talking that shit. Thought he was one of life's poets, one enlightened sonofabitch. Didn't hurt either that back then every college kid wanted to be Che Guevara.

"We were good at what we did. Knew how to forge documents, make new identities. Worked what jobs we could get, spent very little, moved often. Stayed near college campuses mostly; all kinds of free stuff you can get at the bigger ones. Play it right and live simple, you can do well mostly on the labors of others. And that struck us as right. We saw ourselves as ripping off a capitalistic society."

I had been sitting there trying to remember a name, and suddenly it came to me. "Gabriel Lane," I said. "That's who the leader of the Mechanics was. Goddamn! That's you, isn't it, Paco?"

"Long ago. I'm Paco now, and Paco I'll be till they find me somewhere dead in a cheap motel and cart me off to a pauper's grave."

"I think you guys were fucked up," Leonard said. "Doing what you did."

"Our hearts were in the right place, but we got caught up, and pretty soon our hearts shifted. An innocent bystander dies when we bomb some capitalistic bank, some ROTC building, boy that's tough, we hated it, but hey, it happens. The end justifies the means. We'd blow you up for peace and love."

"General consensus is you're dead," I said. "You were supposed to have gotten killed in an explosion, if I remember right."

"I may look blown up," Paco said, "but here I am. Talking and smoking and making your morning bright and gay."

"I'm gay," Leonard said, "but I don't know about the day and what you're doing for it."

"Gay?" Paco said. "You saying what I think you're saying?"

"I fuck men," Leonard said. "Does that clear it up for you?"

"I believe it does."

"You say people died because of what you were doing?" I said.

"That's right," Paco said. "Toward the end we lost some of our own. Cops—or the pigs, as they were popularly referred to then—cornered four of the Mechanics in a house in Chicago. I was out at the time. Making a gun trade. Had two of the group with me. I forget what the rest were doing. But the bottom line is the cops got wind of where we were, hit the house, and killed four of us. Bobbie Remart among them. She was a top radical at that time. On the FBI list right under me. She was kind of my lieutenant. My lover too. After that, things went from being political to being personal."

"You got to feel bad about that shit," Leonard said. "I mean, I killed gooks in Nam, and I was supposed to kill them. Thought I was fighting for my country, doing what was necessary. Still feel that way. But I hate I had to do it. But you guys . . . I don't know."

"You don't look to me like somebody who could do that kind of thing," I said.

"You kidding," Paco said. "I look like death warmed over . . . but I know what you mean. Listen here. You been around, you should know better. Can't judge things by what you see. Look at something long enough, and it'll start to look like something else. Watch me long enough, you might see something you don't see now. Whatever, there won't be any of the old me to look at. That's a guarantee.

"Back then, I thought what we were doing was right. Like you thought what you were doing was right in Nam, Leonard. Felt we were patriots. Least until what happened to Bobbie. After that, I was like something taxidermied that moved. Right and wrong were words. I couldn't see the line of difference anymore, couldn't tell if I was crossing it or not. For me, that line has long been gone and nothing's going to bring it back.

"Anyway, what happened was we were hiding out in this house in Chicago, and I had the Mechanics building a bomb to blow something or another to hell, and I was supervising. I was the one taught them how to build bombs, see, and I wanted to be sure they knew I was still the big daddy. Sasha was the one actually working on it, and the rest of the group were gofering for her. Way they were treating her was making me a little jealous. Sasha was strong-willed and kind of new to us, and the Mechanics weren't turning to me quite as often as before. She was starting to get some of my thunder. I wanted her to make sure she knew her place, you know. I looked over her shoulder, and she was doing all right, working safe, but like I said, I had to be big daddy, and I said something to her about how she needed to work smoother, and she didn't take to it. She was the only one had my number. Knew my ego. Knew how fucked up I was over Bobbie's death. She planned to take things over. I could tell that. She could have done it too. Still had the cause in her. She knew my days as leader were numbered, that I was burned out, just doing by rote. She wouldn't take shit from me. She turned around and started telling me what I could do with my advice, got her mind off what it ought to have been on. Must have let the wrong wires touch. Next thing I knew, the world was bright and hot, full of stone and glass, and I was rolling around in rubble. Ego and explosion had kicked my ass.

"I awoke outside, down in a pit, the house all around me, ears ringing, cold air cooling me down. Somehow the blast had brought the whole place down, and by a goddamn miracle, maybe because Sasha was in front of me, the explosion had thrown me away, caught me on fire, but not burned me up or blown me up.

"I found I could walk. I wandered off, lived under a porch for three or four days, and the people owned the house never knew I was there. When my ears quit ringing, I could hear them come and go and I could hear their TV playing. A dog came under there and slept with me. That's what I did most of the time. Slept. And hurt. Hurt something awful. It was cold then, right at winter, nothing like the way it is here today, but cold. That blast had burned me so bad the weather felt good at the same time it made me shiver and feel sick. It being cold might have been what saved me, I don't know.

"When I got strong enough, I got out of there at night, staggered to a phone booth, busted the phone box open, made it work without any money. Give me a bobby pin, and I can hotwire a jet. I called a man sympathetic to our cause, and he came to get me. When he saw me he gagged and threw up.

"I must have been a sight, all right. Skin burned off, top of my head open. Dirt embedded in my face. An ear gone. Looked like walking, breathing hamburger meat. Way this guy acted when he saw me, I wished the bomb had done me in. Wish that now.

"To shorten it up, he got me out of there and took me to Chub. Chub didn't have what he needed to take care of a case like me. He'd mostly handled gunshots for us before, and those only minor, but here I was with my head wide open, burned over most of my body, and him with just the basic stuff. He did the best he could, I give him that. He kept me there till I was better. Guess I ought to figure I owe him. But I don't. I don't even like the fat fuck. He fixed me up, and I gave him a cause. I consider us even. In fact, from that day on, it didn't take much for me to consider myself even with just about everybody and everything.

"Chub made arrangements for me to stay with some other Movement people. One of them was Howard. He was living in Austin at the time, and I wanted to go back to Texas and rest, get involved again when I felt better. Or so I said, but I knew it was over. The whole dumb dream was through.

"For the next year or so, I went from one sympathizer to the next, being taken care of, passed around like some kind of exotic pet, one of the last of a dying species. The noble, wounded hero who gave his face for the cause.

"Then one by one there wasn't anyplace for me to stay. Harboring a fugitive from the old days was no longer romantic; flirting with the law and danger was no longer fun. People had to take their kids to soccer games and work in the PTA. The really radical people were getting caught. The Weathermen were out of it by then. And that explosion had killed all the Mechanics but me.

"Oh, there were a few die-hards throughout the country that would put me up, but they liked to talk the talk and not walk the walk. On the whole, I was old, bad news. The bullshit times were over. That was it for Gabriel Lane."

"So you're hiding from the law?" Leonard said.

"Not exactly, but I don't want any truck with them. I figure if the FBI thinks I'm alive they're not saying. There was such a mess and mixture of bodies there, they had to have decided it got us all. But I'm not one to take chances."

Paco reached into his mouth, took out his top teeth and put them on the table. So much for his fine smile; it was a fake. The gap where the teeth had been made him look truly horrible.

"Explosion got the real ones. Chub made these for me," Paco said. "Fat bastard knows about medicine, both human and animal, and he knows dentistry. You got to give him that. I've had these teeth, what, twenty years maybe."

He put the teeth back, fastened them to the back molars. "I bummed some, read about me in a few books and magazines, about my death and all, found that what we had done really hadn't amounted to a hill of beans. We blew up some places, killed a few folks, and I've got no face."

"How come you're in with Howard and Chub?" I asked.

"The money. Howard got in touch with me. Thinks now that he's been in prison he's learned some things, that he's an intellectual tough guy out to do some good. Ready to revive the sixties. Power to the people and all that shit. Thinks he's gonna get this money and make some changes.

"But he decides he needs help to do it, and he calls around to some people he knows that know me, and they catch me next time I pass through. And that's no easy feat, cause I go my own schedule. Work till a job plays out or I play out. Anyway, I got the word Howard has something I might want to get in on, something that would do some good. Like the old days. Money was mentioned and I got interested.

"Course, it's really Trudy behind all this. I can see that. I know her type. She hears about this money from Howard, maybe one night after he's put the pork to her, and they're lying there thinking sweet thoughts, reliving the sixties like they do, and she gets an idea about it. Next thing you know, Howard's looking me up, believing it's all his idea. He gets in touch with Chub because he knows him too. We may not be much, but we're all he's got left from the sixties.

"I listen and figure a way to score. Can't do this town-to-town shit labor rest of my life, so I'm in. But not for any goddamn cause."

"And now," Leonard said, "here we all are."

"All right, goddammit," I said. "I bite. What's their plan for the money?"

Paco grinned his false teeth at me. "Trust me. Stay out of it. Take the money, like I'm going to take the money, and go on. I promise you, you'll be a hell of a lot happier."

1 2

Next day the weather cleared up some. It didn't go warm, but part of the meanness went out of it. It was cold with no new ice and no high winds. The sky was flat as slate and the color of chipped flint. Leonard and I took his car down to the bottoms to see what we could see. I wanted to locate the Iron Bridge, find that money, get on with things; go away from this weird winter and Trudy, talk of the sixties and Paco's failed revolution.

Although the house where we were staying was at the edge of the woods, it wasn't the part of Marvel Creek legitimately called the bottoms. The bottoms are lowland with lots of trees, water, and wildlife, and it doesn't start where it used to. Civilization had smashed the edges of it flat, rolled blacktop and concrete over it, sprouted little white wood houses and a few made of two-story brick and solar glass. Barbecue cookers sat in yards like Martians, waiting till the chill thawed out and summer came on and they could have fires in their guts again. Satellite dishes pulled in movies and bad talk shows from among the stars, and dogs, too cold to bark, too cold to chase cars, looked out from beneath porches and out the doors of doghouses and watched us drive past.

Beyond all that, the bottoms were still there. They started farther out from town now but they still existed. They were nothing like the Everglades of Florida or the greater swamps of Louisiana.

Not nearly as many miles as either of those, but they were made up of plenty of great forest and deep water, and they were beautiful, dark and mysterious—a wonder in one eye, a terror in the other.

So we drove on down until the blacktop played out and the houses became sparse and more shacklike and looked to have been set down in their spots by Dorothy's tornado. The roads went to red clay and the odor of the bottoms came into the car even with the windows rolled up: wet dirt, rotting vegetation, a whiff of fish from the dirty Sabine, the stench of something dead on its way to the soil.

Winter was not the prettiest time for the bottoms. Compared to spring it was denuded. The evergreens stayed dressed up, but a lot of the other trees, oaks for instance, went in shirtsleeves. Spring was when the bottoms put on its coat and decorated itself with berries and bright birds that flitted from tree to tree like out of season, renegade Christmas ornaments. Leaves would be thick and green then, vines would coil like miles of thin anacondas up every tree in sight, foam over the ground, and hide the snakes. Considering how thick the vegetation would be in the spring, how many snakes there would be, this bad old winter might come to some good after all. Like making Leonard and me some money.

Still, winter or not, the place was formidable. When I was growing up in Marvel Creek, folks used to say, you hang out down there long enough something bad will happen.

Perhaps. But some good things happened too. I caught fish out of the Sabine and swam naked with Rosa Mae Flood. When I was sixteen, seventeen and eighteen, I parked my car down there and made a motel of my backseat. Made love not only to Rosa Mae, but to other fine girls I remember fondly. Girls who made me feel like a man, and I hope I made feel, at least temporarily, like women.

The clay roads turned to shit as we went, and we had to go slow and easy, and finally Leonard said, "We oughta have something better for down here. Four-wheel drive maybe. We're gonna get stuck."

"Well, we can always go back to town and buy a couple. One for me and one for you. Could get them in matching colors even."

"Just saying we could use it is all."

"We won't get stuck, Leonard. We're the kings of the world. We do what we want, when we want."

"Right."

We eased on and I tried to make out landmarks, but there weren't any. Everything had changed. I had the sudden sick feeling that I had no more idea where the Iron Bridge was than Trudy and the gang. I wondered if anyone knew where it was anymore. All I remembered was that it was not on the river proper, but off of it, and deep down in the bottoms at a place that looked like something out of a Tarzan movie.

"You got some idea where you're going?" Leonard said.

"Of course," I said. "You know me. I never been lost, just—"

"A little bewildered. Save it, okay? I can tell. You got no idea where we are."

"It'll come back to me."

We went on down that main clay road and turned off on a few smaller ones that dead-ended against trees or the edge of the river. Some of the roads were so narrow we had to back our way out. Sometimes we had to back a long ways. Leonard loved that. He knew more foul words than I thought he knew, and I thought he knew plenty.

About high noon we were dipping down over a hill on the main road and there was a sudden sound like strained bowels letting loose, and the car started to slide right.

A blowout.

Leonard tried to turn in the direction of the skid, but the skid didn't care. The ice on those clay roads would not be denied. The right rear fender struck a sweetgum with a solid whack and my seat belt harness snatched at me and pulled me snug.

We got out.

The car wasn't banged too badly. I said, "I think it's an improvement."

"Remind me to knock a dent in your old truck when we get back, you like it so much."

"While you're changing the tire, I'm gonna look around. Looks kind of familiar around here."

"Now the place looks familiar. Got a tire to change, and you know the place like the back of your hand."

"I merely said it looks familiar. I'll be back."

"When?"

"About the time I figure you've got the tire changed."

It didn't look familiar to me at all, but hey, I hate changing tires and tires hate me. I know from all the bruised knuckles I've gotten over the years, all the quick moves I've acquired from avoiding slipping jacks.

My mechanical abilities are simple. I can air up a tire, put water in the radiator, check water in the battery, let water out of the radiator, check the oil and put it in, fill the tank with gas.

Beyond that, I'm an automotive moron.

I walked around a bit, hoping I'd stumble onto something familiar, but nope. I went back to the car and Leonard had the spare on, was jacking the car down.

"Been going well?" I said.

"Now I know why you hang around with a black guy. So in case you have a flat, you got someone can change the tire."

"It's your car."

"Your fault I'm down here."

"All right, you found me out. I like me a black fella to change tires."

"And chauffeur."

"That's right, and chauffeur. I think the ethnics should know their place."

"You so right, boss, and I is proud to serve you."

"Actually, I don't know how to break this to you, Leonard, but I only hang out with black guys when I can't find a Filipino."

"You tighten the bolts. You're not getting out of this scot-free."

He put the jack in the trunk and gave me the tire iron. While I was tightening the bolts, he said, "We could go home. Not even pick up our gear. Just drive out of here and forget all this business."

"We could," I said. I didn't want to admit it, since I was the one who got us into this, but I had been thinking pretty much the same.

"We could go to jail that money doesn't turn out to be the kind of money Howard says it is."

"If there is any money."

"Yeah, if there is any money."

"But there isn't a thing happening at the rose fields now, and I can't think of another line of work we could go into."

"There's always shit work," Leonard said. "It isn't like we're some kind of professionals."

I finished the bolts and put the tool in the trunk, positioned the ruined tire between the oxygen tanks and the diving suits, and closed up. "I leave it to you, Leonard. Whatever you want, that's fine by me."

He thought that over. "Really, any of this familiar to you?"

"I remember part of the road we came in on," I said. "Outside of that, I could be on Venus."

"That's not encouraging."

"No, it isn't."

He thought some more, said, "Tell you what. We'll give it, say, three days for you to start seeing if something's familiar. You see something you recognize, we'll go longer. We find the bridge, maybe we'll look a few days, we still feel like it. Don't come across the boat or signs of it pretty quick, we'll go home."

"Deal," I said.

13

Just before dark we drove back to Marvel Creek, stopped at Bill's Kettle, had a hamburger, bought a six-pack of Lone Star at a cut-rate store, and started back to the Sixties Nest, as Leonard called it.

We found ourselves following the jaundice-yellow Volvo that lived in the yard of the Sixties Nest, and we pursued it to the house and parked behind it.

Howard got out of the car. We kept our seats and drank our beer, observed him like aliens examining an inferior species through the portal of a flying saucer.

He was wearing slightly greasy blue work clothes with a patch over the left shirt pocket. I couldn't tell from where I sat, but my bet was his name was stitched into the patch.

He looked at us a moment and went into the house.

"Looks to have been a tough day at the old job site," I said.

"I know it's got to be the same with you," Leonard said. "I can't make up my mind. Is it him or Chub I like best?"

"They both have a lot of charisma," I said.

We went inside. Paco was sitting on one of the fold-out chairs grinning his false teeth. Trudy was sitting on the couch. She had her legs and arms crossed. She looked as if she could crack walnuts with her asshole.

An unjustified strain of guilt went through me. I felt like a husband whose wife had just found rubbers in his wallet.

The guilt went away when Howard and Chub came into the room. Chub didn't bother me, really. He couldn't help being a jerk. But Howard was a self-made man in that department.

Chub went over to the couch and sat down. Howard crossed his arms and held his ground in the middle of the room and glared at us. His eyes roved a little to his right to check out his audience; the teacher was about to make an example of us.

I wanted desperately to knee him in the nuts.

"I thought there was an understanding that you were working with us," Howard said.

"We forget to punch the clock or something?" Leonard said.

"You don't want any part of what we are, but you said you wanted to do a job. There were things we had to do today, like go to straight jobs."

Leonard looked at me. "Straight jobs, Hap?"

"That's what they used to call square jobs, back in the beatnik days," I said.

"Ah," Leonard said.

"*Straight* is, relatively speaking, a sixties term, still popular today."

"Ah."

"I'm surprised you haven't heard it."

"I've been kind of outta step."

"It's not funny," Howard said. "Chub ran some errands for us. But you two, we had no idea where you were. There were things we needed to talk about this morning. Plans needed to be made. We were all about our business but you two."

"You didn't say what Paco was doing," I said.

Paco grinned even wider. Poor guy. In that face, the fine white teeth made him look a little bit like a sun-dried barracuda.

"I think he's playing favorites," Leonard said. "I hate that kind of thing."

"Paco has earned his keep in the past," Howard said. "I haven't seen what you two can do. But it smells like what you can do is drink beer."

"But can you tell how many we've had?" I said. "Smelling it from over there is good, but I want you to say how many we drank."

"And what brand," Leonard said.

"No use trying to talk to them when they're like this," Trudy said. "They'll go on until you get tired or mad. You can't reason with the fools."

"Fools?" Leonard said. "Now that's rude."

"I'd as soon the two of you pack up and get out," Howard said.

"We'll decide when we get out," I said.

"And if we stay," Leonard said, "we still won't report to you. You're just some guy we don't know, that's all."

"Besides," I said, "while you been fretting about what we been doing, we've been down in the bottoms looking for the Iron Bridge."

"And?" Chub said.

"We didn't find it," I said. "We're going to give it three days. I don't come up with it, maybe we will get out. You can go your own way then. We won't tell on you or anything. You'll have our blessing."

"Anything look familiar?" Trudy said.

"No," I said, "but it's been a long time since I been there. But I can solve all this easy. I can just ask someone. A classmate, an old-timer. It might be thought odd if one of you asked, not being from here. I can claim nostalgia, wanting to look around at the old growing-up place."

"I'd rather you not," Howard said. "It'd probably work out all right, but I think if we can get through this without it being mentioned anywhere, better off we are."

"I agree with that," I said. "I'm just saying what we can do if things get too difficult. I leave, and you'll have to ask. And even if you're told, you'll never find anything down there. You'd need a guide. Then you'll be tying one more person into it you don't know."

"As Leonard pointed out," Howard said, "*we* don't know each other."

"True," I said, "but I sense something special about you and me and Trudy. We could be one big happy family."

Howard uncrossed his arms. I could see the patch on his shirt pocket. It said FLOYD.

"You guys are pushing your luck," Howard said.

"Please don't start that again," Trudy said. "I don't want to see Hap or Leonard hurt you, Howard."

Howard looked at her as if she had just sliced his nuts with a knife. "He might not be so lucky this time," he said.

"Luck hasn't got a thing to do with it," Leonard said.

"Why don't you guys arm wrestle?" Paco said.

"Don't you start in too, Paco," Howard said. "You're starting to sound like them. What you've done doesn't hold you forever."

"Well," Paco said, shaking out a cigarette, "I hate that."

"Floyd?" I said.

"What?" Howard said, then it dawned on him. "It's just a shirt."

"Man with no pride in his name or shirt, it's hard to know what to think of him," Leonard said. "He could be anybody and not even care. I'd want my own name on my shirt."

"Me too," I said.

14

I stood on the front porch and looked out at the night.

Everyone was in bed but me. I had turned in but the cold and my thoughts wouldn't let me drift. I had the uncomfortable feeling that Trudy and the gang were planning something stupid. I had no idea what, and had decided to follow Paco's advice about not knowing, but I couldn't help but think about it. Because of that, I had got up, pulled on my shoes and coat, and gone outside to think.

It was cold and clear and the moon and stars were bright, and their lights rested in the yard like puddles of gold and silver paint and wound through the trees like gold and silver ribbon.

I tried to find Venus. There was a time when I knew where to look. I couldn't remember if it was visible this time of year or not. Once things like that were important to me, and I knew some answers.

I read in a book that primitive men could see Venus in the daytime at high noon with the naked eye. In fact, sailors as late as the 1600s could do the same, and they guided their ships by it. Now the ability was no longer needed, or desired, and modern man could not see Venus in the daytime.

I was somehow distressed by that. Hell, I couldn't even see the bastard at night.

I gave up on Venus and let my mind smooth out. I absorbed the night and the moonlight and watched my breath turn white against the dark. That was about all the thinking I was willing to handle.

I took a deep breath of chill air and went inside, tossed my coat on the gutted armchair, sat on the couch, and picked up a book Chub had left on the coffee table. It was one of those books that explained how everyone could profit from analysis. It was written by an analyst.

Marking his place was a faded black and white snapshot. It was of a big black-haired guy, somewhere between thirty-five and forty-five, kind of handsome, with wide shoulders and a smile full of big white teeth. There was something about him that made me think of someone who had ran a few pigskins between the goalposts, and now ran a few deals past his competitors. On his right was an attractive, well-dressed blond woman who looked like she had trained to be the Queen of England, and might have been, had the job not been taken.

Pushing his way between them, as if not really invited, was a blond kid of eleven or twelve with enough meat on him to loan to two others. He was smiling, but the smile wasn't much. His was the face of a kid picked last for football games and told to go long, the face of a guy not really asking for a lot, and getting less.

The kid was Chub, of course, and I felt sad looking at him. I turned the photograph over. Written on the back in a young hand was *Mom and Dad and me.*

Maybe the picture meant something to him—a slice of a good moment, when he thought he'd grow up to please his parents and be something other than a fat kid. And maybe I was full of shit, and it was just a marker.

I had just started reading the book because I was bored enough to jack off with a fistful of barbed wire and roses when the hall door opened gently and Trudy came into the room.

She was wearing a red tee shirt and nothing else. It fit tight. Her nipples poked at the fabric like the tips of .45 casings, and it stopped high on her thighs and made her seem all legs. Her hair was tousled and she looked tired and somewhat older without her makeup. She looked good though. She smiled at me, closed the door softly, leaned against it, said, "You, too?"

"My mind's racing," I said.

She nodded at the book. "Learning anything?"

"It's all anal and sexual. Talk about shitting or fucking and you reveal yourself immediately."

"Do you, now? I was going to slip into the kitchen for some milk. Think I'll wake Leonard up?"

"If he were straight, you just walking by would wake him up. I'm surprised the whole house isn't awake. Dressed like that, you ought to ring like a bell."

"Want some milk?"

She always did take compliments well.

"I'll take some milk."

She brought back two small fruit jars filled with milk, handed me mine and sat down beside me. I couldn't help but put my arm around her.

"You really do pick at Howard," she said.

"I don't like Howard. He's a prick."

"He isn't so bad."

"Guess not, you're sleeping with him."

"I like him. I used to love him. Not like you, but I loved him."

"Uh-oh, here we go." I took my arm from around her.

"Put your arm back, silly."

She crossed her legs high and the tee-shirt went way up. She wasn't wearing underwear. I put my arm around her again.

I said, "Didn't you forget something?"

"Howard tossed them somewhere."

"That's not what I wanted to hear."

"Truth."

"Sometimes a little white lie is better."

She set her glass on the coffee table and kissed me on the neck.

"You going to go through all the men in the house tonight?" I said.

"Is that supposed to make me mad?"

"Yep."

She kissed me on the neck again. "You're the only *man* in the house."

"Shit, Trudy."

"You like me saying that, don't you?"

"If I believed it, I'd like it more."

"Like you said, sometimes a little white lie is better."

I smiled.

"Let's go for a ride, Hap."

"Now?"

"Uh-huh."

"You might get a little chilly, lady."

"Just a minute."

She got up and eased the door open and smiled back at me before she went into the hall. After she closed the door I thought about her going to the room she and Howard shared, tip-toeing about, looking for her panties and her clothes. I had looked through the house earlier, just to look, and their room was a small thing with a mattress on the floor and a messy pile of blankets and some Coke cans tossed about.

At the other end of the hall Paco and Chub shared a slightly larger room. Chub slept on a saggy box frame bed in the middle of the room and Paco had a cot in a corner. The room had very little in it. A chair with clothes tossed over it and a small box of Chub's books, all of them on subjects designed to be read at gunpoint.

Less than five minutes later she was back. She was dressed in a blue denim work shirt, jeans, scuffed black work shoes, and a thick red and blue jacket. She looked like the best-looking lumber-jill alive.

She held up a set of keys.

"The Volvo," she said.

"Will Howard mind?"

"Of course."

I pulled on my coat and we went outside and got in the Volvo, Trudy behind the wheel. We backed out and the ice in the drive crackled under the tires. We drove to the highway and started toward Tyler, which was about twelve miles away. The car heater worked slowly, and the car was as cold as a meat locker. The highway was smooth with hardly any ice. I guess road crews had been at work salting it. There were splashes of gravel for the really bad spots.

Trudy reached for me and I slid over and leaned my head against her shoulder and she kissed my cheek. She held one arm around me as she drove and I smelled her perfume and the slightly stale wool of her coat.

I felt good and a little foolish. There was enough of the old male culture about me that I felt positions should have been reversed. I hoped no one saw us.

We drove like that for a long time. Finally Trudy said, "I wanted to go for this drive because I wanted to talk."

"About what you people have planned?"

"You people?"

"You know, power to the people and all that."

"Really have become a cynic, haven't you? God, but I miss the old Hap Collins."

"Did you miss me the most while I was finishing up my prison term?"

"You never have got past that, have you?"

"Let's say it's the sort of thing that weighs on a fella's mind."

"I did miss you, okay?"

"I like the way you showed it."

"I never claimed to be perfect. I'm sorry it happened like that, but it did, and that's that. I can't undo it, so let's leave it. And the plans we have isn't what I wanted to talk about. I thought I might work up the courage to tell you something about myself you don't know. Something you ought to know. For old time's sake."

"What kind of something?"

"Something pretty awful."

15

"I killed Cheep," she said.

"Our bird?"

"Yeah. Could you move on your side of the car while I talk about this?"

I moved to my side of the car.

"It's complicated, Hap. Cheep was not only our bird, he was a symbol of our relationship."

"Sounds to me like you been reading Chub's books."

"I been thinking is what I been doing; thinking for years. Trying to figure why I'm no good at relationships. I go into them full tilt, mean for them to work, but I can't maintain. You were the best. I had a shot there. But I messed it up. I mess them all up. You see, I got to have my white knight. I know better. Be your own person, and a woman is a person too, and all that shit, but I got to have my white knight. And if the man I'm interested in isn't a knight, I try to make him one. I send him on a quest, and soon as he's no longer on the quest, I lose interest in him, and the cause I've sent him on. I may get interested in the cause again, but I got to have my white knight with me if I'm going to do anything. I see my knight as going out there and doing what he's doing not only for the cause, but for me. I suppose it makes me feel loved. Important. Understand?"

"What's this got to do with Cheep?"

"I'm coming to that. But when the cause really takes the knight—in your case prison—I feel cheated. Like it's not for me anymore. Things come apart. I want to start over, get a new knight. But I couldn't do that with you because of Cheep. Just a bird, I know, but he made me feel tied to you. Other things wouldn't do it, the cause, the love we shared, but the bird was a living reminder. He wouldn't fly away. Depended on me completely. And I couldn't just leave him. He wouldn't have lasted any time in the wild, and in fact would have suffered. But I didn't want to start life anew with him. He reminded me I was a failure at things. Relationships, what have you.

"So I filled the bathtub with water and took Cheep and held him under till he drowned. It didn't take long. He didn't suffer. But I still think about it. I carry that goddamn bird's ghost on my soul like a weight.

"But when I did it I felt good. Not that Cheep was dead, but that I had made a strong decision without anyone's help, or without me leading someone else into doing what I wanted. It should have been a turning point. But I didn't really understand why I did what I did at the time. I knew I wanted to be free of something, but I wasn't sure what. You were my first major love, but on a smaller scale, with boys in high school, couple in college, I had already established a kind of pattern. Building someone up so they could be special, and since they were special, and they loved me, it made me special. Against all odds, we two . . . that sort of thing. You see, killing Cheep was killing a symbol."

"Cheep might disagree."

"But the sense of freedom didn't last. I fell back into my old ways. I found a new knight and let him lead, and when he led away from me, I went knight hunting again, and again. I understand all that now. What I'm saying, Hap, is that I'm ready to kill a bird again. This time, the bird is the old me. I'm going to drown that bird and be a new person. Someone who believes in herself. In idealism for its sake. Not as a symbol of worth, or love. I want to be a woman who doesn't need a man to put out front and pretend he's leading and suffering for me, his fair-haired damsel. Don't have to say, 'Look at my man go.' *I* can go. Come hook or crook, I can see things through."

"Jesus Christ, Trudy. You been doing some major rationalizing here is what you been doing. You're not learning to be independent. You're realizing how selfish you've always been is all, and you're justifying it with some bullshit self-analysis, like Chub would do."

"Think what you want."

We were silent for a time.

"This thing you're going to see through," I said. "It sounds serious."

"Let's say I'm serious. I'd like to have you with us, but I don't need you the way I used to need you. I don't need Howard either."

"Don't need us, how come you got us?"

"I want your help. But I don't have to have it. Not the old way, as my knight. All I want is to believe in something so strong, that belief and my own inner conviction carry me. Like those monks who set fire to themselves to protest the Vietnam War. I want to have that kind of dedication."

"They had dedication, all right. But they also got burned up."

"It's all gone bad out there, Hap. Worse than the sixties, because now no one cares. Someone's got to do something, even if what they do is nothing more than stirring the soup. We could start people thinking. They're all so apathetic. So what if the ozone layer is being eaten away by pollutants in aerosol cans? So what if people are starving on our city streets? Why have government funding for AIDS? It's a disease for queers, right? People don't even vote anymore, because they know it's all a lie, Hap."

"Don't forget the destruction of the seals." I said. "The whales? The sparrows like Cheep?"

"I did what I had to do, Hap. It was a terrible thing, but sometimes you have to do terrible things so you can make progress. Sometimes you do something terrible so some good will come of it."

"Trudy, you got to grow up sometime. You can't take the world in to raise. No one can."

"I feel sorry for you, Hap. You got nothing left inside to hold the dark away."

When we got to Tyler, Trudy turned around and we started back.

I said, "You seem to be avoiding telling me exactly what it is you have planned."

"I thought I'd tell you tonight, Hap. But I've decided not to. You might try and mess it up out of spite."

"I may disagree with you, but I'm not spiteful."

"You might be. You've changed. Could be I don't know you good as I thought. I wanted you with us, but I think now you should do your job and take things as they come to you."

We didn't cuddle and kiss anymore. We didn't even talk. Trudy turned on the radio. It was an all-sixties station. Percy Sledge sang "When A Man Loves A Woman," followed by the Turtles singing "She Only Wants To Be With Me." Good stuff, wrong moment. It was depressing.

We got back to the Sixties Nest, and I was about to get out when she reached across and put her hand on my thigh.

"You couldn't have changed that much, Hap. You were so . . . noble."

I put my hand on hers, suddenly wondered if this hand was the one that had held Cheep under. I wondered what else this hand was capable of. I took hold of it and put it on the seat between us.

"Watch it, that's knight talk. . . . You've changed too, Trudy. You may have the willpower and dedication you always wanted, but I think maybe you lost something in the process."

"I see it as a gain."

"Whatever. I think for you and me, there's been too much blood under the bridge."

I got out of the Volvo and went in ahead of her, went to the back porch and took off my coat, socks and shoes, rolled up in my bedding.

I heard Trudy come in and go through the hall door, then I didn't hear her anymore.

I lay there listening to Leonard snore and tried to force myself to sleep for a few hours, but I'd go in and out, and when I came out I would remember bad dreams.

Dreams that ought to have been funny, but weren't. Like this soft, feminine hand holding me by the throat, pushing me down into a tub of water. My mouth was open and I had a beak instead of lips and I was blowing bubbles.

Then I was floating face down in the water, my back covered with feathers, the water in the tub red as blood.

1 6

Next morning I waited in my sleeping bag until Trudy and Howard were off to work. I didn't want to look either of them in the eye. Didn't want to see the look of disappointment she would give me, the look of pain Howard would have. He probably woke up in the middle of the night, found her gone, and thought we were out banging one another silly until the wee hours of the morning.

I think Trudy would have wanted him to think that. I wish that was what had happened. I wish I had never learned the truth about Cheep.

Someone had bought a few groceries the day before, so Leonard pan-toasted a couple slices of bread and we spread them with butter and had some bad leftover coffee the texture of syrup.

Outside the day was cold, but still clear. We drove to the bottoms and began our game plan.

What we did was simple. We drove down the main bottom road until we saw a cutoff we thought the car could handle, and we took it.

Sometimes the cutoffs circled back to the main road, or met up with another little road.

When a road dead-ended at the woods or river, or was just too muddy to drive, we got out of the car and walked awhile, hoping I'd see something familiar that would lead to a tributary or creek or some little outflow of water that might be the home of the Iron Bridge.

Mostly we walked and Leonard cussed the brush and rotten logs we stepped over. I think he did it to irritate me. I'd never known the woods to bother him before. I think he wanted to remind me he thought this whole thing was stupid and he was humoring me.

I tried to ignore him and listen to the cries of the birds and the splashing sounds coming from the river. Those sounds made me think of great fishing days and channel cats, the catfish they called the trout of the Sabine. Gunmetal grey, lean and graceful with pointed heads and wide, forked tails. And there were the bigger cats that swam along the bottom of the river or laid up between the huge roots of water-based trees. Some called them bottom cats and others called them flatheads. They were big, brownish rascals, sometimes fifteen feet long, weighing up to a hundred pounds, narrow-tailed, with a wide head and a mouth big enough to suck up a child. And there were stories that they had.

Certainly there were gars in there that had bitten children and pulled swimming dogs under for their afternoon meals. They didn't call the big ones alligator gar for nothing. Six feet long, lean and vicious, they were the barracudas of fresh water, beasts with angry racial memories of lost prehistoric seas.

And now and then, there was the real McCoy, the alligator. I had never known them to be plentiful along this stretch of the Sabine, and growing up I had seen only one in the river, and that one from a distance. Another I had seen big and complete, lying dead in the back of a fisherman's pickup out front of Coogen's Feed Store.

To the best of my knowledge, they were hibernating. Hoped so. Rare or not, it only took one to punch your ticket. They weren't the sort of critters minded eating a man in a dry suit, oxygen tanks and all.

Definitely the cottonmouth water moccasins, the meanest snakes in the United States, were hibernating, and that was a relief. Winter, even one bad as this one, was not without its charms.

We scouted around like this until noon, then drove into town, bought some bread, sandwich meat and beers, drove back and found a little road that terminated at the river bank, sat on the hood of the car and had lunch.

We didn't talk much. We watched the brown water roll by and spread out in a dirty foam where the river widened down to our left. "In the spring it would be great to come here and fish," I said.

"Yeah," Leonard said.

Another half hour went by.

"Guess we ought to get back at it," I said, totaling a beer.

"Yeah."

We walked along the edge of the bank and the wind picked up and brought a damp chill off the water; the sky had gone grey as a cinder block.

We went until the bank became nothing more than mud and gravel and was hard to keep our footing on. We were about to turn back when I saw a great tree split wide from lightning, its blackened halves lying one on the bank, the other partially in the water.

I studied it.

"That used to be a big tree," I said.

"Good, Kemosabe. Pale Face no miss fucking thing. Him know big trees from small trees. Pale Face one smart sumbitch."

"It used to have an old tire swing hung from a chain. The swing was over the river."

"You're saying you remember something?"

"We'd bail out of it into the water, then climb up and do it again."

"We're near the Iron Bridge?"

"No, I just remember the tree and the swing."

"But it's a landmark to help you find the bridge?"

"Probably not. I remember the tree, but can't put it into relationship with the Iron Bridge. I know we used to come here is all. The Iron Bridge is on the side of the river we're on, though. Bridge goes partway over a creek that shoots off the river on this side. The tree helped me remember that."

"That's something," Leonard said. "You remember that much, means we can spend all our time looking on this bank."

"It's not real close to the river, as I recall. It's down this creek I'm thinking about, and quite a ways."

"Meaning the creek you can't find?"

"That's the one."

"So, Dan'l, what do we do now?"

"Any more beers?"

"Nope."

"Guess we keep looking."

17

Back to work we went, driving those back roads and excuses for roads, and it was late afternoon, maybe two hours before dark, when we drove around this curve and I happened to look out and see this rusty metal pole, and, bam, there was an explosion in my memory centers. At first I couldn't place what had exploded, but around the curve we went, and the debris from the explosion rose to the top of my memory and began to tumble into something identifiable and I said more calmly than I felt, "Stop the car."

"You're smiling," Leonard said. "You got something, right?"

"Turn around."

He had to drive a ways before we could find a wide enough place to get the car turned, and when we got back to the curve and the pole, I had him pull over. We got out, and I took a look. My smile got bigger.

"When we used to come down here this pole had a metal sign on it," I said. "Probably rusted off the bolts and's under all these leaves and pine needles, a few years of dirt. Sign said something about this piece of land belonging to some oil company or another. I don't remember exactly. But by the time we started going here, there were bullet holes in the sign and it was no longer valid. The oil company had long since lost its lease on the place, and it had reverted back to the county, or the State of Texas, or whoever owns it. But the little road for trucks and equipment was still here, worn down and grown up some, but still usable."

"It's not here now," Leonard said.

I looked where I remembered the little road being. The trees were scanty there, relatively young. In spots there were patches of dirt mixed with old hauled-in gravel, and neither trees nor weeds had found support there. If you studied hard enough, you could see where the little narrow road had wound itself down into the woods toward the water.

"I think this was the road Softboy and his boys took after robbing the bank," I said. "They made all these pretty good plans, but the dumb suckers saw water and assumed they put their boat next to the Sabine."

"But it was the broad part of the creek that flows under the Iron Bridge?"

"Yep."

We pushed limbs aside, stepped through the browning winter grass, and then followed the faint curves of the old road. When we came to water, we were at a spot as wide and deep as the Sabine at its best. It was easy to see how someone who didn't know the river could mistake this for it.

"If they had a car down here and ran it off in the water," Leonard said, "reckon Softboy would have done it right here, don't you think?"

"Yeah, but it might not be there now. Over the years, the floods and swellings, even something the size and weight of a car could move, if only an inch or a foot at a time."

"Thank you, Mr. Wizard."

We went walking along the bank. The undergrowth turned thick and grew out to the water. There was little room for footing. Sometimes we hung on to limbs and roots and dangled out over the creek, pulled ourselves along the steep bank like that until we found ground again. It was tough work, and even cold as it was, we worked up a lather.

The creek eventually turned narrow, just wide enough and deep enough for a boat to go on. I recalled it widened again at the bridge, then, not far beyond that, narrowed enough to jump across, and went like that a long ways.

We got past all the undergrowth and came to the second

widening of the creek. There was plenty of bank to stand on now. The water was dark and spotted with stumps and lily pads. Great trees leaned out from the shoreline and spread branches over the water thick as macramé, dripped vines and moss. Past all that, where the water was less dark and less riddled with stumps, was the Iron Bridge.

Half a bridge, really—what was built before the money played out. It sagged, and was covered with vines and moss. The metal, where it was visible, had gone red-brown with rust.

"Why would they build here?" Leonard said. "Back a ways they could have thrown a bridge across in an afternoon."

"They were going to widen all this, entire Sabine and its tributaries, I think. Make one gigantic river out of it. They had, as the Baptist preachers say, grandiose plans. Thought they'd be getting so much oil they'd be using river barges. Tools and machinery coming from the northern end of the river, oil in barrels heading South. But it played out before they got started good. There're abandoned wells all through these woods."

"You know," Leonard said, "I'm a wee bit excited. If there's a car down there, just might be a boat with money in it. Finding the car would be a way of checking. We got an hour before dark. What do you think?"

"Now's as good a time as any," I said.

We went back to the car and opened the trunk. The tanks were well packed in foam rubber so they wouldn't bang together and blow us to hell. And they could. They were highly explosive.

Leonard got in the backseat first and took off his clothes. He had this tube of grease for bonding the dry suit to the flesh, and he rubbed the grease all over his body and pulled on the suit. He got out of the car and put on the tanks and mask.

Then it was my turn.

I hated the grease part.

We put our clothes in the trunk, got a fifty foot coil of thin rope out of there, and went down to the water carrying our flippers.

Leonard fastened the rope to his belt and went in first, and I fed the rope out to him, keeping just enough slack in it.

After a few minutes, he came out of the water and shook. He

took the regulator out of his mouth and pulled his mask up. His face looked gray.

"No car?" I asked.

"Fuck the car," he said. "Goddamn." He sat down on the shore and took in some deep breaths and shook. His teeth chattered.

"Chilly, huh?"

"Whoever called these bastards dry suits had to be kidding. I got water all inside, and it's cold, buddy boy, I will assure you. My balls are the size of grapes."

"Before you went in, or after?"

"Funny. Look, it's deeper there than you think."

"I remember it as deep," I said. "Used to fish and swim here."

"There's a mild suck hole too."

"That I don't remember."

"It isn't bad, but it could trick you. It's about where I came up. Damn, I'm freezing."

"I won't be down long."

"Not telling me nothing I don't know. You think it's cold up here, this is the tropics compared to that water. And it's dark. So dark, you'll come up and it'll seem like the goddamn world's bright enough to be on fire."

"If you had listened in your science classes, Leonard, instead of beating your meat under your desk, you would know that it takes more energy to warm a square inch of cold water than it does a square inch of cold air. And absence of light makes it dark."

"Just listen, smartass. You're gonna feel numb at first, little confused. Think you're getting too disoriented, don't wait till you're so messed up you don't know what you're doing, come up, or yank on the rope and I'll help you up. I'm not jacking with you, Hap. Water like that will screw you around. Play some serious tricks on you."

"Gotcha."

I put the rope through my belt and tied it loosely in case it got tangled. Leonard took hold of the other end but kept his seat.

I pulled the mask down, put the regulator in my mouth, pulled on my flippers, and eased under the water.

It didn't hit me for a second, but when it did I felt a wave of blackness and paralysis all over. The cold went right through the suit like some kind of freeze ray. It was a feeling like you have when you get something cold on the wrong tooth, only it was my entire body.

It was all I could do to make myself breathe the Nitrox in my tank.

The wave of blackness passed, though, and I could feel something like cold bug feet creeping through my dry suit; it was water seeping in, of course.

I got organized best I could and swam down deeper. I could feel Leonard letting out the rope.

I couldn't have gone far before I touched bottom, but it seemed to take forever. My head, heart, and lungs felt pregnant with ice. I couldn't see anything. It was muddy from all the rain and overflow from melting ice. I crawled along the bottom like a crab.

I wanted to swim to the surface, but somehow couldn't make myself do it. It took all my concentration to breathe from the respirator, keep in mind where I was, what I was doing, and that air and daylight were not too far above my head.

It came to me eventually that I was looking for a car. That struck me as funny. A car in the river. Cars belonged on the highway. I had a car once. I had a truck now, but I had a car once. Leonard had a car. Lots of people had cars. Or did cars have people? It was an interesting thing to think about. If I'd had a pad and pencil, maybe I'd have taken a note to consider that later. No, I couldn't see well enough to take a note, and paper wouldn't do so good down here. I'd have to remember about the cars and sort it out later.

I felt a tug, as if wires were attached to me. I couldn't figure it.

Leonard pulling the rope?

No. That was the other direction.

Did I have another rope on me?

No, I didn't think so.

The suck hole. I was near that and it was pulling at me.

Had to think. Okay. Underwater. Got air. Cold as the tip of a penguin's dick. Looking for a car. Honk, honk.

The suck hole was pulling me. My arms were weak, and I didn't feel as if I could swim. I went with the suction. It wasn't bad, but it was enough to pull me. It seemed important that I do something, but I couldn't think what it was.

Then the river bottom went away and there was water and

tugging. I was over the suck hole. I had swam over and into suck holes and out again in my time, but I wasn't this cold then. Beer would keep good in this water, but you'd want to drink it in a warm place. In front of a big fireplace would be nice. Maybe something to eat with it. I really preferred my beer with food.

Something was keeping me from going down.

The rope. It had gone taut. Leonard had me. Seemed to me that was supposed to be good, but I couldn't be sure.

But wait a minute. I was in the suck hole and my feet were touching something.

This wasn't a very deep suck hole. I wondered how wide it was. Maybe I could put a picnic table down here and have that beer and a sandwich on it. But I'd have to wait until summer. Wait a second. You can't drink beer underwater. Sure can't eat a sandwich. It would get flimsy. And taste like the water. The water was dirty, too.

It was so goddamn dark. Had I been down here so long it was night?

What were my feet touching?

The rope was tugging at me. Leonard was pulling me up.

Hold on here. I didn't ask to be pulled up. I'm thinking down here, goddammit.

I got hold of the belt and unfastened it and let it go. The rope wasn't pulling me anymore.

I bent forward and touched with my hands what my feet had been standing on. It was something flexible. I got hold of it with both hands and held on to it and my feet floated straight up. What I was holding came loose and I began to float up.

Let's see, did I want to float up?

Now something had me, had me hard. I wanted to fight against it, but I was holding this thing in my hands and I didn't want to lose it.

Why didn't I want to lose it? I could let it go and fight back.

I thought about that, but by the time I decided to let go I was on the surface and Leonard had his arm under my chin and was pulling me toward shore. The sun was very bright. It wasn't so cold. I could see trees and sky between their limbs. My hands felt numb. I was still holding my prize. I thought I should let it go. All I had to do was have my brain tell my fingers, "Let go, you sumbitches."

I let go. I was lying on my back. What I let go of was on my chest. A monster bent over me. No, Leonard. He pulled back his mask. He took the respirator out of his mouth. He was calling my name, but it sounded as if it were coming from far away. He was calling someone else too. A person named Shadhad. No, wait a moment. That was shithead. Could he mean me?

"Answer me, shithead. Are you all right?"

"I think so," I said.

"You took off the belt and the rope."

"Did I?"

"You did."

"Couldn't think clear."

"The water, smartass. I told you. Too cold. We haven't got top equipment here and we don't really know what we're doing. . . . You're okay?"

"Uh-huh. But you can forget finding any car down there."

"That right?" He picked something off my chest, wiped it with his hand a couple of times and held it in front of my eyes.

It was a rusty license plate.

We took off the swim gear and used some Kleenex from the glove box to get the grease off of us, then we dressed and drove into scenic downtown Marvel Creek. We had a couple of Lone Stars and a hamburger at Bill's Kettle. Afterwards, we splurged and had chocolate pie and coffee.

When we finished, Leonard said, "Course, it could be some other car."

"How many cars are gonna end up in the middle of a creek like that? And that suck hole is wide enough and deep enough to hold a car during floods and water risings over the years, and when the river gets low, bet that spot's covered with enough water to keep the car out of sight."

"What we got is a license plate, though, not a car."

"It was hooked to a car. It came off because it was rusted."

"You know, the boat could really be out there. And with a little luck, the money."

"Lot of luck. By the way, did I thank you for saving me?"

"Not nearly enough. More humility on your part would be good. I went down there without a rope and pulled you up at great risk to my own life."

"How great a risk do you think?"

"Real great. I fought the suck hole and the cold and you. I can't think of anyone braver."

"Or more modest."

We went on like that until we were tired, then we found we didn't want to drive back to the Sixties Nest. Didn't want to sleep on a cold back porch with butane in our snouts. We got some beer and some cheap wine and rented a room at a rundown motel and stayed up most of the night telling lies and a few sad truths that we hoped the other would think were lies.

Leonard talked about his grandmother, and how fine she was, how he loved her, then talked about his dad, who beat him until he was fourteen and he turned on the old man and kicked his ass, and the old man went away and never came back and his mother died of diabetes and shattered dreams. A stint in the army seemed all right to him. He didn't talk about Vietnam. He skipped that part, and of course I'd heard it all before and he knew it, but a drunk doesn't care about what's been said before, he cares about now and about how he feels, dragging that stuff up is like putting on a good old blues song you've heard a hundred times. You know the words, but it still does you good.

He moved on to other things. Sad history became glad lies. He talked about his dogs, about this one—long gone to her reward, of course—that was smart as Lassie. Could jump through hoops and run for help. Another glass of wine and he might have told me how she could drive a car and smoke a cigar, maybe work a couple calculus problems.

But it didn't get that far. He got limp and paused too long and I told him how I'd lost some plans. About how the future that was not the future I'd wanted. He listened good, like he always did, and what I said was all right. He was with me, knew this line of patter, nodded knowingly in all the right places, way I had with his much-heard story about his good grandmother and his runaway father and his dead mother. Then I told him about Trudy and Cheep, sneaked it in like an inside curve ball. I was looking for a little sympathy there. Figured I deserved it.

"You dick," Leonard said. "I told you that bitch was poison. Paco told you. Everyone knows what she is but the guys in love with her. Maybe I wasn't queer I'd love her too. But from my perspective, she's just a bitch with some patter, and you're an A-one jackass that can't tell a hard-on from true, sweet love. Goodnight."

The thing I like best about Leonard is his sensitivity. Tell you one thing, though, I'd listened to his last goddamn dog story cum lie. He could tell it to the bushes.

Next morning, dull-eyed and slick-tailed, we drove out to the Sixties Nest, ready to deliver our news.

18

After we told them what we found, it took two days to get everything together, make a few plans. They gathered up chainsaws and axes and brush knives and an aluminum boat, and somehow Howard talked his boss into letting him borrow the wrecker for a Sunday afternoon.

His boss must have found him considerably more charming than Leonard and I did. At my worst, I wouldn't have pissed on him had he been on fire, and at my best, I would have stomped the flames out.

So we went down there on a cold-as-hell Sunday, the sky all funny-looking and threatening rain, and we took the tools and cut a path for the wrecker to get down to the creekbank. It wasn't much of a path, but by cutting a tree now and then and chopping out some undergrowth, the wrecker, one of those big things with monster tires, was able to get through. We put out a few fishing poles here and there as a disguise, but I thought that was damn silly. Anyone came along and saw all the work we'd done to get that wrecker in, saw our wet suits, and believed we were just dropping a few lines off cane poles was going to have to be a lot dumber than a stone.

Still, that's what we did. All of us but Paco. He was gone as he often was, and nobody offered an explanation, and I couldn't have cared less.

I girded my loins and prepared to put on the dry suit. I didn't want to go back down there, but I knew if I didn't, Leonard would, and I couldn't let him do it just because I was a chickenshit. Not that I hadn't considered it. He offered, and it was tempting, but I made it clear the first round was my baby. My dad always said that if something scared you, thing to do was to face it head-on. Saved yourself a lot of sleepless nights that way. Course, it was an attitude that might get you killed. I wondered if dear old Dad had considered that possibility.

I rubbed myself down with the grease and pulled on the suit and took hold of the wrecker's hook and cable and went down to the edge of the water.

Leonard came over, said, "Sure you want to do this?"

"Course not."

"But you're gonna?"

"Yep."

"Get in any kind of trouble, I'll come get you."

"How you going to know if I'm in trouble?"

"I won't let you stay down long, oxygen tanks or not. You don't come up pretty quick, I'll go down there and get your ass."

"I know that's your favorite part, Leonard, but bring the rest of me up with it."

"Deal."

I pulled the mask down and Howard let out some slack on the cable. I went into the water, swam directly toward the suck hole. It obliged by dragging at me, and I went with it. It was as dark as before down there, and just as cold, and I had to work not to get tangled in the cable. A mild feeling of panic moved over me, but I put my mind on my business and swam with the current. It wasn't as bad this time. I could feel the pressure of the cold against me, but I must have gotten myself greased better this time or my suit put on tighter, because no water was seeping in.

When I was in the suck hole, I turned with my feet up and felt to see what had given up the license plate. It sure felt like a car bumper. I ran my gloved hands over it some more. Yes sir, what we had here was a genuine automobile. I got the hook attached by feel, hoped it was secure, grabbed the cable, and followed it up rapidly. It took only a few seconds, but when I broke the surface, I felt as if I had been down forever.

Howard got the winch going. It whined and pulled taut, paused, started whining again. Before long our catch broke the surface. I couldn't tell what color it had once been, because it had long since adopted the gray and green of the creek bottom's mud and mold. The rear window was mostly busted out, and what glass was there was flimsy-looking, as if it were not glass at all, but crinkled plastic. The tires looked like black chamois rags wrapped around the wheels. The windows were down, to help it sink no doubt, and water and mud the texture of a sick man's shit rushed out of them.

When it was on the bank, we gathered around it.

"It's a car," Howard said, "but is it the right car?"

"Softboy said he had some partners," I said. "Check for bones."

Time and fish would have long since taken care of any bodies in the car. Bones might have washed off or been carried away by larger fish, but if the car had gone into that suck hole and lodged there early on, just maybe they had been preserved. And if not, there might be some other evidence there that would tie the car to Softboy.

The doors wouldn't open, so Howard got a bar and went to work. When he popped them, mud oozed out. Trudy and Howard got shovels and started scraping. It wasn't too long before Howard found a skull. He wiped it on his sleeve until we could see that it had a large hole in the left side and a smaller one in the right.

Trudy dug around in the backseat until she came up with another mud-covered skull. She brought it out on her shovel and Howard took hold of it and scrubbed it with his sleeve. This one had a small hole in the forehead, and at the back, one the size of a fist.

"I got a feeling Softboy lied about his partners," Leonard said. "Those are close-up shots. Small one's the entry wound, big one's the exit. I think he finished them himself. Money'll make you do things."

"He didn't seem that way," Howard said.

"Well, things aren't always what they seem," Leonard said.

"One thing, though," Howard said. "He told the truth about the car. And you know what that could mean."

We had the fever then. I tried to figure where Softboy might have wrecked the boat, and decided the best thing to do was to check both sides of the bridge in the deeper water, see what we could come up with. Leonard and I took turns going in. It was surprisingly deep on either side of the bridge and I thought maybe they had dredged there, preparing to dig the great waterway that never happened.

We swam along the bottom, and at first we panicked at everything we touched. Some of it was the usual garbage: cans and bottles and plastic containers that had once housed soaps or colas, all manner of crap that belonged at the dump and not in the water. Sometimes there were big things and we hooked the winch cable to them and Howard hauled them out. There were a number of fifty-five-gallon drums full of who knows what, and tires and wheels, the occasional transmission or lawn mower, and of course the ever popular irregular shaped rock.

No boats. No pieces of boat.

I was less fearful of the water now, and I tried to keep that in mind. Over-confidence is the way to give your soul to the devil an inch at a time. The dry suit was pinching me some. Water was starting to seep in, and I could really feel the cold. We dove and we dove, and by late afternoon I was exhausted.

We had found neither money nor boat nor boat pieces, and Leonard and I came out of the water and out of our drippy suits and dressed in our clothes for a little warmth and a break. Paco showed up with sandwiches and coffee, and he and Howard went off down the bank to talk about something or another.

The money fever was fading. I thought about how long ago the boat had gone down, and all that could have happened to it over the years, and a mild depression moved in. If it had broken up when it wrecked, it might have gradually been carried away, and the money with it. It could have long since made the sea.

Trudy had been ignoring me. She was about her business of sorting through the junk we'd pulled up, hoping to find some overlooked fragment that might resemble a boat. I couldn't help but watch her, the way she moved was tantalizing.

There was this mound of dirt and vines and scraggly growth not far from the water's edge, and she took a break and went to lean on it, and the way she leaned, with her pelvis thrust forward, put a pain in both my heart and my groin. And I think she damn well knew it.

She shifted her hips without looking at me, making it seem pretty natural, but not quite, and suddenly she moved away from the mound and put her hand to the small of her back and rubbed, then reached out and rubbed at what had poked her. "This looks like a bone," she said to no one in particular.

I went over and could see the edge of something poking through the mound of dirt. It looked more like a rock to me, but even if it was a woolly mammoth bone, I wasn't greatly in the mood for paleontology. I felt she had used it as an excuse to get me over there so she could persecute me with her presence.

She ignored me and began to dig around the edges of the thing and pretty soon it was clear what it was, and it was considerably more exciting than a rock or bone.

It was the blade to a boat propeller.

She looked toward the bank where Howard and Paco were standing, staring out at the water.

She said, "There's something here."

Howard and Paco came over. Leonard and Chub showed up.

Howard looked at what was there, said, "Oh man, that means—"

"Means it's a boat propeller," Leonard said. "But not necessarily *the* boat propeller."

"How would a boat get up here?" Chub said.

"Water might have put it here and receded," I said. "Since no one would have looked for the boat down here, it might have been sitting here, slowly gathering dirt over it."

"Or," Paco said, "what we may have here is a propeller blade and a mound of dirt. But one thing's certain. There's a boat in there, we're not going to talk it out."

Shovels came out then, and we were on that mound of dirt like worms on a corpse. Howard and Paco and Leonard on one side, me and Chub on the other, Trudy with a trowel working at the propeller. Chub was so frenzied he nearly whacked me twice with his shovel handle, and he nipped my ankle with the shovel blade once. I had to threaten to do him damage to make him watch what he was doing. But we were all a little frenzied, and when Trudy uncovered a large hunk of outboard motor, even more so. We dug and we dug and the sun went down and the cold became colder, but I wasn't aware of it until I paused to relax and felt the sweat cooling on my face. The cold air cut at the rims and insides of my nostrils and sliced down my throat and hissed in my lungs and made them throb like a wound.

But I kept digging.

At some point Howard turned the wrecker toward us and pulled on the highbeams so we could see. We started digging even faster. We came to some thick twists of roots and we got the axe and Leonard elected himself Paul Bunyan. He cut at them with hard, precise strokes and the roots flew up and out, and we went back to digging. Finally Howard's shovel hit something that sounded unlike root or rock. He dropped his shovel and dipped his hands into the dirt and came out with the crumpled top of an aluminum cooler.

We all paused and looked at it. There in the cold highbeams and the splotchy moonlight, it had as much majesty as a silver shield. "Could be, could be," Howard said, and then we were digging again, really digging. The mole population of the world couldn't have been any busier. Wooden fragments that might have been boat pieces were found next. They were as crumbly as artificial fireplace logs.

Then Howard's shovel hit something else. He lifted out a long aluminum canister cracked in the middle. We all looked at it. I felt as if I had suddenly been filled with molten lava, that a little ice had gone out of my soul. Lost years were on the verge of being regained. Possibilities went through me, grew heads like a Hydra. The fact that this money might be partially mine for the taking, that it was stolen and illegal, filled me simultaneously with ecstasy and guilt, like I'd have felt if my mother had ever caught me jacking off to a girlfriend's picture.

Howard tried to loosen the lid, but couldn't. He finally resorted to bending it at the break to work it apart. He managed that and wads of something dark fell out of it. Trudy was suddenly there with a flashlight and Howard grabbed what had come out of the canister and squeezed it between his fingers and cussed.

I took hold of it too. It was paper, probably the money; it was black and the texture of wet tissue. Another year or so, it might make good garden mulch.

"There's supposed to be several containers," Trudy said. "They can't all be broken."

"Yes they can," Leonard said.

His words were anvils dropping on our heads. I felt a little dizzy and empty, as if hungry, but there wasn't any food that was going to fill this gap. The boat and the canister had given us a moment full of dreams, and now those dreams threatened to grow wings and fly south and die among the bones of all our dreams.

Yeah, that money could make up for a lot of missed ambitions, but without it we were nothing more than a batch of losers, standing cold and silly, empty-handed on the muddy bank of an unnamed creek.

We went back to digging and sifted through some more wood and some metal and plastic and some chunks of glass. Eventually we came up with another canister. This one wasn't broken open. Howard got a screwdriver and a wrench and with shaking hands went to work on the lid, popped it off.

Inside was some money. It was in a plastic bag, in bundles, and looked in good shape. Howard tore open the bag and the money fell out. Trudy grabbed it, unfolded it, dropped to her knees, starting counting.

I could hear her breathing, all of us breathing. We were puffing out white, cold smoke, chugging like little trains trying to make a last bad hill.

It took a long time to count that money, longer than I would have imagined, and we all stood there watching those bills go off that wad and out of her hands and onto the ground, and after what seemed enough time for continents to sink beneath the waves and new ones to rise up out of the sea on the shoulders of volcanic eruption and for new life-forms to come into existence, she said, "A hundred thousand."

With the sharp voice of greed, Howard said, "There's got to be more than that."

We went at it again, and before long uncovered another canister. Again the money was counted—this time we all took some of it and made little piles—and what we had in this one was just short of two hundred thousand. All of it was in good shape. We dug till we found two more canisters. Both held money. One had a few damaged bills on top, but the bulk of it was okay. We leveled the mound. No more money.

We counted what was there, added it together. We had just over four hundred thousand. Trudy took the money and rolled it into tight little rolls and put it back in the bags and wrapped the bags firmly with some tape she had and put the spoils in the two best canisters.

"That's a lot less than a million," Howard said.

Though it looked as if my dream was going to be a smaller one than I had hoped for, I was glad to have anything. In fact, I felt a little giddy. I looked at Howard. He nodded. I said, "Seems to me this is a good tax-free haul. Might be another canister or two in the water, but personally I've had it. This could be all there ever was. Talk about money is like talk about fish. Both grow in the telling."

"Me and Hap," Leonard said, "we'll take our share now. I want to get back to my dogs and Hap wants to get on down to Mexico."

Howard looked at Paco, then Chub and Trudy. "Now, huh?"

"That's right," I said.

"Well," Howard said, "just a minute." He stepped back and opened his coat and reached inside and pulled out something and pointed it at us. Even with his back to the headlights and there being only an occasional snatch of moonlight through the trees, I could see well enough to make a fairly accurate guess at what he was holding.

A flat little automatic.

19

Turned out they all had guns. When Howard pulled his, they produced theirs. It was pretty disconcerting, all those people standing there holding cheap automatics.

Howard drove the wrecker. Trudy drove the mini-van. Chub drove Leonard's car and Paco hung over the front seat and pointed a .32 automatic at us. The bottoms raced by us in black bands and twists of oak fingers and pines shaped like dunce hats. The moon crept through it all and faded in and out with the rolling of the clouds.

I didn't look at Leonard. I could sense he wanted me to, but I didn't want to see that well-deserved I-told-you-so look.

"You guys are some kidders," I said to Paco. "I thought they wanted the money for a cause and you just wanted the money. Turns out you're really in this together, and you all just want the money."

"No," Chub said. "Not true. We have a purpose. Thing is, we require it all. We thought there would be more and we could give you some. But little as there is, we can't afford it. We made a pact that if there wasn't enough for our needs, we'd have to appropriate your share."

"It's needed for a buy," Paco said.

"Drugs?" I said.

"Guns," Chub said.

"Guess you're going to give them to some South American revolutionaries to fight their capitalistic oppressors," I said. "Something like that."

"Something like that," Chub said. "Only we're not giving them to anyone. We're the revolutionaries."

"Oh shit," I said.

"Great," Leonard said. "Bozo the clown and his clown buddies with guns. Probably gonna have live ammunition too."

"We need all the money," Chub said, "because the weapons we're buying are state of the art. Right Paco?"

"Sure," Paco said.

"Paco said if we found this money, he had connections and he could get to them right away. People he's worked with before. Right, Paco?"

"Right."

"He's been checking with them all along, in case we got the money. He's got them to quote us some prices. We theorized that we'd need quite a lot of them and plenty of ammunition, and we'd need money for when we went underground, so we could make payoffs, buy food, supplies, that sort of thing. Enough for us to get established before we started robbing banks."

"Banks?" Leonard said. "You're going to rob banks?"

"Not for the money. Of course, we'd have to have some of it to finance things. But we'll give a lot of it to supporters of politically correct causes."

"Politically correct," Leonard said. "I love that."

"We didn't really intend to cheat you, but with so little money there, and our plans being as ambitious as they are, we had to. It's nothing malicious or personal, it's a matter of priorities."

"Ah," Leonard said. "I see. For a moment there, I just thought we were getting fucked."

"We're going to have to keep you awhile," Chub said. "Until we make the buy and go underground. Let you loose now, you might spill the beans. We don't want anyone knowing about us just yet. Soon everyone will be aware of us, and we'll be glad for it."

"I wouldn't tell a soul," Leonard said. "Think I want the world to know I got snookered by you goofs? Some revolutionaries you're gonna make. You couldn't find your shitters with both hands."

"Paco's done this sort of thing before," Chub said.

"Yeah," Leonard said, "and all he got out of it was a burned-up head."

"Fooled *you*, didn't we?" Paco said.

"I'm afraid you did," I said.

"We have to do something," Chub said. "This country is rapidly going the way of fascism. The spirit of the sixties can't be lost—"

"Christ," Paco said. "I'm going to join the fucking capitalists you don't shut up."

2 0

Another cold night, but not as cold as it had been at the Sixties Nest. The heat worked well here and there was some of it in every room, and the rooms were slightly larger and better-looking, much less depressing. Logs crackled pleasantly in the living room fireplace. Still, it wasn't comfortable. We'd slept sitting in armchairs, and to add insult to injury we were in Leonard's house, Howard and Trudy having spent the night in Leonard's bed, except when they took their turn sitting on the couch with their guns, watching us, looking as if at any moment a great shootout was inevitable.

They had taken their watch together about midnight. I could see the clock on the fireplace mantel, could hear the bastard tick the minutes away as if dropping water on my head. Paco was sleeping somewhere in the kitchen and Chub was wrapped in blankets on the floor near the fireplace.

For lovers, Trudy and Howard didn't look at each other much. They sat on the couch at opposite ends. There didn't seem to be any electricity between them. They had become, at least in their minds, hard-nosed professionals in the last twenty-four hours.

They had all changed. With us prisoners, our captors had taken on an unconscious swagger. Maybe they hadn't wanted this to happen, us being out of step with their plans, but since it had, they were eating it up. It gave them reason to tote their guns. They were having a taste of revolutionary foreplay. Orgasm was anticipated.

I nodded in and out, watching Trudy and Howard watching me and Leonard, and came completely awake and reasonably rested to the sound of Chub groaning. Trudy was toeing him awake. "Your turn," she said. "There's coffee. Don't go back to sleep."

"Don't talk to me like a kid," Chub said. Coming awake like that, he'd momentarily forgotten the lessons of analysis. How he wasn't bothered by anything.

"They got no respect for you because you're fat," Leonard said.

I looked at Leonard. I hadn't noticed him coming awake, and he had awakened as grumpy and sarcastic as ever. No wonder he didn't have any lovers. Who'd want to wake up to Groucho Marx every morning?

"You get thick," Leonard continued, "everyone treats you like you're a talking pork chop."

"You don't bother me," Chub said. I doubted that. Earlier, before he bedded down, during one of my awake moments, I had seen him standing near the living room window, examining his reflection in the dark glass, and I could tell from the way his shoulders slumped that what he saw was not what he wanted to see. He got up, washed his face at the kitchen sink, drank a cup of coffee, got his gun from under his pillow, and took to the couch.

"We're going for a walk," Trudy told him.

"Outside?" Chub said.

"No," Howard said. "We thought we'd circle the fucking couch."

"Just asking. It's cold out there."

"Say it is?" Howard said.

"You're all jumpy," Chub said. "Come on, we're in this together." Chub's face wore the same sad look it had in that photo of him as a kid. He so desperately wanted to be treated like an equal, he couldn't help but act inferior.

Howard took a deep breath. "Yeah, well listen, we get back, we'll help you take them for a bathroom break."

"I got a big dick," Leonard said, "but it don't take but me to hold it while I piss."

"We wouldn't want you to be lonely," Howard said.

"What if we got to pee now?" Leonard said.

"Hold it," Howard said.

"Is a number two, a doodie, any different?" Leonard asked.

"Hold that too," Howard said.

Leonard looked at me. "He's just too tough. When he talks I get this little rush in my loins, don't you?"

During this exchange Trudy had disappeared into the bedroom. She came out now wearing a bundle of clothes, her big lumberjill coat topping it off. "Put something warm on," she said to Howard.

He went into the bedroom and came out a few minutes later bundled as heavily as she was. They went out the front door. I closed my eyes and dozed.

Next time I came awake, it was to the sound of the back door opening and closing.

Trudy and Howard came in through the kitchen, red-faced from the cold. The bottoms of Howard's pants were spotted with wet dirt and the toes of his shoes were tipped with it. Trudy looked as clean and desirable as ever, even decked out like a little she bear in her winter coat.

I looked at the clock in spite of myself. Two-forty-eight. Time flies when you're having a good time.

Howard got his pretty little automatic out and pointed Leonard to the bathroom. When Leonard finished, I took my turn and went back to my chair.

It was three A.M.

Moving right along.

Leonard went right back to sleep. He even snored. For me it was more nodding in and out. Once I awoke and Chub had gone back to his place on the floor and Paco was on the couch, gun in his lap. There was a saucer on the arm of the couch and it was full of cigarette butts and there was a cigarette in his mouth and a cloud of smoke hung over his head. He looked a little twitchy. It was the first time I'd seen him that way. There were beads of sweat on his wrecked face and that studied cool he'd had was on vacation. When he saw I was awake he called some of the cool home, smiled, gave a slice-hand wave and picked up his gun with the other hand.

I thought about jumping him, but I also thought about getting shot. If Leonard were awake, I might signal to him, and we could jump him at the same time. The bastard couldn't get both of us.

Or maybe he could. And if he only got one of us, I didn't want it to be me, and I assumed Leonard felt the same way about himself. And if we did take him, it probably wouldn't be without a noisy struggle, and that would bring the rest of them awake, and they all had guns.

I gave Paco the foulest look I could muster, twisted in my chair, and was about to close my eyes when Trudy came out of the bedroom. She was carrying a flashlight, wearing her lumberjill outfit again, only this time with less bundling under the coat.

Paco looked a question at her.

"Can't sleep. Going to take a walk."

Paco nodded.

She went out through the kitchen. She was a walking kind of gal this night. I closed my eyes and slept. It was Trudy coming back that woke me. She wasn't all that loud, but I wasn't that deep in sleep either. She came in red-faced from the cold again, pulling off her brown cotton gloves. She came over to the edge of the couch, looked at Paco, then stared at me for a long, hard time. I studied her in return. The bottoms of her pants and the toes of her boots were crusted with clay and there were a few pieces of gravel stuck in the clay at the front ridge of her boot like ugly gems on hard red velvet. The great Hap Holmes deduced she had been out walking along the edge of the creek, where Leonard had tried to build up his land to keep it from washing away.

She tired of trying to stare me down—which was good, I was about to look away—and walked behind the couch and into the bedroom and closed the door.

"She's still got the hots for you bad," Paco said.

"Save it," I said.

The clock showed a little after five.

I didn't go back to sleep again. By six, Howard and Trudy were both up. Trudy had already showered and was wearing one of my shirts with a clean pair of jeans. Everyone else had on what they had worn the night before. Howard got guard duty. The rest went into the kitchen and scrounged through Leonard's stuff for breakfast. Leonard awoke in time to see them using up his coffee, his bread and butter, and most importantly, his vanilla cookies. Losing the cookies really bugged him. He had a passion for them, kept them hidden even from me. Paco found them by accident and put them on the table so they could be had with coffee, and though we were offered some, I could tell it was no fun for Leonard to get his own cookies from assholes.

I had picked up tidbits of information here and there, listening to them talk when we were at the Sixties Nest, and now here at Leonard's, and I had a good idea of their general, if not specific, plans. With the exception of Paco, who was tight-lipped and unreadable, they weren't secretive about the general stuff. They had brought us here because the guns they intended to buy were to be bought someplace outside of LaBorde, and neither LaBorde or that place were excessively far from Leonard's house. Last, but not least, Trudy said Paco had contacts in LaBorde that would help them go underground. They weren't ex-movement people, they were drug runners. But the method for getting lost from the mainstream was the same no matter what your purpose. After all, Paco had done it for years. They only had to follow his lead.

I hoped they would do what they were going to do and get it over with, then let us go. I didn't want to spend another night sleeping in a chair. The rose fields seemed like a better career today than yesterday. I wanted out of the picture. I wanted to toss away its frame and knock down the wall it hung on.

But when we were out of this mess, I was uncertain what I'd do. If I went to the police, I had to tell them about the money I'd helped find. I could lie my way around it for a while, but if they caught one of the others, the truth would come out, and I might end up viewing the world from behind bars again. Maybe Huntsville prison this time, but a prison just the same. The difference in their exercise yards would not be of enough interest to make the time appealing. And even if I didn't mention Leonard, one of the foiled revolutionaries might. Leonard wouldn't like prison any better than I had or would again. Yet, if I said nothing, innocent people might die during one of the group's holdups, and no matter how I might rationalize it, that would be on my head.

It was not an exciting morning. Paco used Leonard's phone a couple of times to mutter a conversation at someone, and with the exception of Howard, who was sitting on the couch with his gun, guarding us, we were essentially ignored.

Finally Trudy came over and sat on the couch, reached under her (my) shirt and took the gun out of the waistband of her pants and said to Howard, "I'll watch awhile."

Howard got up and went to the table, laid his gun beside the bag of cookies, opened the bag and went to work. I could almost feel Leonard flinch while Howard ate. Leonard sure loved his cookies.

I smiled at Trudy. It was not a nice smile. "You're all jackasses," I said.

She smiled at me. It was not a nice smile. "Whatever you think, Hap. You and I aren't connected in any way anymore. It's just not there. What you say doesn't matter to me. You don't do what we say, try to get away before we're ready to let you go, try to screw things up, we'll shoot you. Wound you if we can. Kill you if we have to. Don't think our past will keep me from pulling the trigger myself. Understand?"

"All too well."

"What are you going to do with us, and when?" Leonard said.

"Paco's got to make another call, then we'll know when and where to meet our contacts, know better what we're going to do."

"Why not have them come out here and we can have a party?" Leonard said. "They can finish off my cookies."

"Better yet," I said, "leave us here. Cut the phone lines or something, let the air out of Leonard's tires. Go your way and leave us be."

"If I knew everything would go smooth, I would. But I want you two with us until the moment we've got the guns and we're ready to go underground. We have some kind of delay and you two are free, you warn someone, then we could get caught before we're ready to make things work. And if our game plan doesn't go right, something about this buy sours, we can have here for a home base for a few days till we put something else together. I want us prepared for any emergency. When it all works out you'll be with us, and if it doesn't happen here, we'll let you out some place where you won't be able to get to a phone too quickly. Not someplace so isolated you'll freeze to death or be too miserable."

"We sure wouldn't want to inconvenience you none," Leonard said.

"Then Paco's going to take us to meet our underground

connections. New transportation has been arranged. We'll ditch the van, and—"

"And the rest is history," I said.

"We'll try to make a difference," Trudy said.

"Take the money and give it to the goddamn whales," I said. "This is stupid. You with a gun? Think about it."

"I have. I've been for gun control all my life, and now here I am with one. Soon to have more. But I've given to the whales and I've given time and what money I could get to most everything. This time I'm giving myself, and I'll make a difference."

"Hap told me about the bird you drowned," Leonard said. "I think that makes you ready for anything, a stone killer."

"Oh, shut up, Leonard," Trudy said.

"Serious now," Leonard said. "You could call yourself the Ice Birds. You know, like the Weathermen or the Mechanics, only you can be the Ice Birds on account of you're bad enough and mean enough to drown a sparrow. Shit, I want in. I'll drive and you shoot."

"It's all comedy to you two," she said. "Exist from day to day, watch out for yourself and each other, and that's it. You're not contributing to anything beyond your moment. If it doesn't affect you immediately, then it's of no consequence."

"Sounds right," Leonard said.

Trudy leaned back into the couch and held the gun in her lap. She said, "You're hopeless."

"That may be," Leonard said. "But what I'd like to do is call a friend who's been feeding my dogs, tell him I'm home and not to come over. I don't want you Ice Birds—"

"Don't call us that."

"—getting touchy and shooting an old man for one of the bureaucratic, capitalistic pigs that run our society. And I'd like to go out and feed them. Anyone else tries, Switch will take their face off. You can bring your arsenal along so I don't run off."

"Call him," Howard said. He had been listening on the sidelines, and now he was waving Leonard out of his chair with his automatic. "Any tricks, though, and you could get yourself or Hap hurt."

Leonard made the call. It was quick and simple and friendly. No codes were passed. He went out and fed the dogs and Paco and his gun went with him. The morning crawled by like a gutted turtle. About noon Paco made a call. When he quit mumbling into the phone he said to the others, "They got a place and a time for us to meet. Sounds okay. Think we can get this over with pretty quick. Get the money, and let's do it."

21

We went in the mini-van. Chub drove. Paco sat in the front seat beside him. Trudy and Howard sat in the middle seat and turned around and pointed towel-covered guns at me and Leonard in the backseat. Outside the weather had turned wet with icy rain and the wipers whipped at it like a madman trying to tread water.

"Can we stop for burgers on the way?" Leonard said.

No answer.

We caught the loop and took it around LaBorde, out past the city limits to a stretch made up of long metal storage buildings, and finally the old Apache Drive-In Theater.

It was no longer in operation and would possibly someday become the site of a number of rectangular aluminum buildings the size of aircraft hangers. Before TV hit it a left, and some years later video cassettes finished it with a hard right cross, it was the place to go, but now it was condemned junk.

The great old Apache Indian head figure that had stood atop the marquee was gone, probably stolen, but the marquee itself was there, high up on its metal poles. There were breaks in it and the red letters mounted there were few and left a cryptic message: ED N HE ST.

We drove past the marquee, past the pay booth, to what used to be the entrance. There was a plywood barrier now. Kids had spray-painted pictures and graffiti on it. The pictures were the usual hairy vagina and dick and balls and most of the sexual suggestions were misspelled. At least when we were kids and did that sort of thing we spelled *Fuck* with a *c* in it.

"Honk the horn," Paco said.

"What?" Chub said.

"They said honk the fucking horn."

Chub hit down on it and held it.

"Just once, dammit," Paco said.

The plywood wall shook and slid back. When it was halfway across a woman appeared from behind, got at the other end and shoved it some more.

As we drove past her, I saw that she was in her late twenties, tall—over six feet—and dark-haired. Attractive. Wearing a jogging suit with a blue jean coat over it. The coat couldn't keep you from noticing she was a bodybuilder. She looked a trim one seventy and her muscles hopped like rabbits when she moved.

I looked back and saw that she had hold of the plywood and was backing up, pulling it into place.

I glanced at Leonard, and he raised his eyebrows.

I took a deep breath. I could feel my hands fluttering on my knees. Howard's Adam's apple was working slightly and Trudy was watching me intently, her breath audible.

"Park here," Paco said, and pointed at the concession stand. We parked and got out. Howard and Trudy took the towels off their guns. More professional that way. The cold rain beat on our heads and drenched us to the bone. I found myself looking at where the old drive-in screen had been. I wished it were ten years ago, and I was here for a movie.

Paco went into the concession by himself, came out a moment later. "Come on."

We went in. It was dry inside but very cold. There was all manner of rubbish on the floor: beer cans, condoms, old popcorn bags, candy wrappers and a pile of turds that might have been human or animal.

We went past what had been the concession counter and into a room that had a faded sign above it that read OFFICE. Inside there was an old cheap desk made out of what they called pressed wood, but was little more than hardened cardboard. On the desk was a battered black porkpie hat and a frayed black umbrella. Behind the desk was a man sitting on an upright soda drink crate, his feet and legs were visible through the opening beneath the desk. He was long and lean, dressed in black slacks with hightop black tennis shoes. His red and black plaid shirt poked out over a vanilla windbreaker. In spite of this light attire, he didn't look cold. Quite the contrary. He had black hair cut short and greased and combed back. He wore a pair of thick-lensed glasses with square black frames. The nose bar and the left wing of the glasses were wrapped with thick white tape. The eyes behind the glasses seemed huge. They were black as his hair and only slightly less oily-looking. He smile and showed us he was missing some teeth in the right side of his mouth. His face was slightly flushed and pimpled with sweat. He looked as if he were running a fever that was trying to break.

We were all stuffed in the little room and now the muscular woman came in, shook her wet hair like a dog. She had one hand in the pocket of her coat. She leaned in the corner, pulled a leg up and bent it so that the sole of her foot was pushed against the wall. Her face held no more expression than a wax dummy.

"Hey, the revolutionaries," said the man behind the desk. "Qué pasa. How the fuck are you?"

"We're all right," Howard said.

"Glad to hear it," the man said.

"We'd like to deal quickly," Howard said.

"Sure," the man said. "But let me introduce myself. . . . Ah, fucked up. Ladies first." He nodded at the Amazon. "That shapely piece of meat is Angel. Me, I'm Soldier. I want you to remember that, know who you're dealing with. Case things don't go down the way you like, you can come to me and say, 'Soldier, things aren't to my satisfaction.' And I can say, 'Fuck you.'"

I glanced at Leonard. He looked as uncomfortable as I felt. Howard and Trudy still had their guns but they weren't pointing them at us anymore; they held them against their legs.

"Do you know what I'm saying here?" Soldier said.

Howard looked at Trudy, and I saw his left cheek jump. Trudy's lips made a thin white line. Chub moved over near the wall Angel was occupying. He was between her and the desk. Paco moved to the right of Soldier. He had his hands in his coat pockets and was looking at the dirty, paper-littered floor.

"Nobody knows what I'm saying?" Soldier said.

"No," Trudy said. "We want to deal for the guns. That's all we want. You give us the guns, and we give you the money. We got to see the guns first."

"You do." Soldier looked at Paco. "Hear that, they got to see the guns first?"

"I hear," Paco said.

"You got guns," Soldier said. "All you got guns, 'cept for this one,"—he pointed a finger at me—"and the nigger. Right?" He looked at Paco. "They're the dumb assholes helped find the money, aren't they? That right? I got 'em picked? I know I got the nigger picked. He's the only nigger in the bunch. Black man, you called him. Black my ass. I know a nigger when I see one."

"Yeah," Paco said. "That's them."

"My folks brought me here when I was fifteen. Moved down from Jersey to get here where you spear-chuckers know your place. And you're worse here. Everything's gotten so goddamn . . . What's the word, Angel?"

"Homogeneous," Angel said.

"That's it, goddamned homogeneous. You got your best Ku Kluxers up North now. Southerners, they've come to think a nigger's all right. Turns my stomach."

"Hating a person because of their skin won't solve anything," Chub said.

"Shut up, Chub," Paco said.

Soldier looked at Chub in surprise. It was as if he had just seen a miracle. "Who the fuck asked you to talk?"

"Not everyone feels like you do," Chub said.

"Not now, Chub," Paco said.

"You shut up too," Soldier said, pointing a finger at Paco. He shifted it to Chub, said, "Angel, move."

Angel stepped toward me. I saw a snubnose .38 come out of her coat pocket. I glanced back at Soldier. He stood, picked his hat up, took hold of the .45 automatic under it, pointed it at Chub and fired. The back of Chub's head went by me in a gray and red flash, hit the wall where Angel had stood. Chub bent his knees slowly, went down until he was supported on them, fell back with his face to the ceiling. The rest of what was in his head ran out like sewage.

The sound of the gunshot throbbed against the room, and Soldier, the .45 still pointed where Chub had stood, said, "Anyone makes to use their gun, I'll kill 'em. If not me, Angel. Not Angel, Paco."

We looked at Paco.

"That's the way it is," Paco said.

22

"Yeah," Soldier said. "That's the way it is. Now play real smart, don't give me any nigger lectures, and let Angel collect your guns. Pretty please?"

Angel merely took hold of the barrels of the guns, one at a time, tugged gently. Trudy and Howard were so stunned they let go without realizing it. Angel tossed the guns on the desk, went over and opened Chub's coat and pulled his out of his waistband. I couldn't help but look at those open, bugged eyes of his, that small hole in his forehead, the puddle on the floor where the back of his head touched. No more analysis for him. No more worries about being the inadequate fat boy. I hoped at some point I had said something nice to him, more for my sake than his.

Angel tossed Chub's gun on the table with the others.

Soldier nodded at the guns. "These are for shit. You dips wouldn't have known guns had I had them. I leave here, I leave that shit right here on the desk. . . . You see, there never were any guns, or any goddamn underground. There was just Paco and he's been talking to me, and he knows me and knows I got a line on some deals, and he wants to make big bucks. Get out of the chickenfeed, you know. The big score, and all that shit. Besides, who but me is going to hire the ugly sonofabitch for something big, huh? No offense, Paco. Fire'll do that to you. Make you like scrunched . . .

What's that wrapper paper, Angel? They put it around Twinkies, that kind of thing."

"Cellophane," Angel said.

"That's it, that's the stuff your face looks like, Paco."

Soldier turned back to us and moved the sight of the .45 along the side of his jaw. Our eyes went to him and his gun and back to poor Chub. A gun and a dead body will hypnotize you, especially with the echo of the shot still ringing in your ears, the coppery smell of blood and shit stuffed full in your nostrils.

"Those are special expressions you're wearing," Soldier said, and he smiled at Trudy and Howard. "Got your goats, didn't I? Came in here all ready to deal, dragging prisoners along like you're somebody tough, and now you're all my prisoners. And I ain't got gun one. Don't think I can't get 'em, now. I can. Could. But I don't deal them much anymore. They're a hassle. Easy to get caught. Dope's easier. But Paco, he comes to me, says he's got something easier than that, got some real dumbasses on the hook that I don't got to do business with you. Just got to be here to take your money. And you know what's best for you, we'll get on with that part right now, because I don't take shit. I'm like my old man. He didn't take none of it neither. Old lady mouthed off at him, whamo." He made backhand motion. "We kids didn't mind, whamo. Hey, see this ear." He turned his left ear to us. "See how it's kind of cauliflowered. Nothing creepy, now. Not like old Paco there, but a little fucked, you know. Old man did that. Beat me within an inch of my life. Deserved it. I was disrespectful. . . . Look here, I'm going to take that money now. Which one of you's carrying?"

I looked at Trudy. She was staring without seeing. Howard looked at her, then back to Soldier. No one said anything.

"Nobody's talking to me here," Soldier said. "Someone better talk to me real soon, or I'm going to have to get someone's attention. I'll start with the nigger, then the nigger's pal. Paco, what's his name?"

"Hap," Paco said.

"Hap. Old Happy Kind of Guy . . . Listen, talk to me. I'm going to get the money anyway. I can shoot you and search you. But hey, I'm easy. I'd prefer you show a little respect here and give it over. I'm big on respect. Know what I'm saying?"

"We want the guns," Trudy said, and her voice was surprisingly firm.

Soldier smiled. "What's that? The guns? You want the guns?" He looked at Paco. "She wants the guns." He turned back to Trudy. "Bitch, I told you, there aren't any guns. No bang-bangs. Not even any bullets for you to throw. You see, it's like this. You give me the money, and I don't blow your brains out. That's the deal, see, and that's all the deal there is." Soldier lifted the automatic and pointed it at Leonard. "We'll start with the coon, he'll be missed the least. We work up from there and end it with the woman."

Howard said, "We didn't bring it with us."

"Say what?" Soldier said. "What're you talking here? Got in a hurry going out the door and forgot the money? Huh? That the story? Hey, you better talk to me, asshole."

Howard's Adam's apple seemed to be plugging his vocal cords. "We don't have the money with us."

Soldier put the automatic on the desk and looked at Paco. "What's this? There some money or not?"

"There's money," Paco said. "I saw it."

"You wouldn't fuck with Soldier, would you?"

"I saw the money. I told them to bring it."

"You told them. You didn't see them bring it, though, right?"

"No, but there's money. Ballpark of four hundred thousand."

"All right, you . . . What's your name?"

"Howard."

"Right. Howard. About this money you didn't bring with you."

"We . . . me and Trudy thought we ought not to bring it. We thought things might not work out . . . that we'd have to bargain. The guns might not be right, and if we didn't have the money with us, we . . . well, we . . . "

Soldier pointed a finger at Howard. "You'd have a lever. Am I right on that? Talk to me."

"That's right," Howard said.

"Then," Soldier said, picking up the automatic, "you could jack with old Soldier, and he'd say, oh gee, you don't like this deal. Well, we'll set it up again. Fix it to your satisfaction. Man, you must have fallen off the . . . What kind of hay truck am I going for here, Angel?"

"The proverbial," Angel said.

"There you are. You must have fallen off the proverbial hay truck, Howard, my friend. You see, I don't have to deal."

"I brought five thousand of it," Howard said. "We thought that could be a down payment if things weren't just right. We were trying to be cautious. We thought of it last night."

Soldier turned to Paco. "They thought of this last night. They didn't tell you? I mean, you're supposed to be one of them and they didn't tell you?"

Paco shook his head.

"It was a precaution is all," Howard said. "In case of . . . in case of a double cross."

"A double cross. Hey, I don't like not being trusted, see. It's disrespectful."

"We thought there'd be guns," Howard said. "Just thought that we might get skimped on the number and the quality. We'd read about that kind of thing."

Soldier nodded his head. "Read about it, uh-huh. Well, how much you say you brought?"

"Five thousand."

"That's not piss in a bucket, Howard. Tell him, Angel."

"That's not piss in a bucket," Angel said.

"You'd have to pay me more than that to fuck your sister if she had six feet of legs and a pussy like a velvet clam. That's nothing. I make that in a day, Mr. Howard. You're wasting my time. Give me the five thousand."

Howard dug in his jacket, came forward and gave Soldier the five thousand, went back to stand by Trudy. Soldier put the automatic on the table and thumbed through the money. "Five thousand, all right. This'll be part of my share. That okay with you, Paco? Angel?"

Neither answered. It wasn't meant as a real question.

"Now, here's what we're going to do," Soldier said. "You're going to tell me where the money is, Mr. Howard."

"Leonard's place," Howard said. "We buried it."

"I see, buried it," Soldier said. "What I ought to do here is shoot the lot of you, 'cept Howard. Then you and me, Howard, we can go dig up this money."

"Be less messy to take everyone and go get it," Paco said.

"You say something, man?"

"I don't want to kill anybody 'less I have to," Paco said. "I've done it, but just when I have to."

"I say you have to, Paco, you have to. You think I didn't have to kill that asshole a while ago? That what you're thinking? A little bloodshed could have been avoided here? I'll tell you, that asshole had no respect. That's the difference between you and me, Paco. I demand respect."

Soldier sat down on the soft drink crate and looked at us. "What about you, girlie?" he said to Trudy. "What you think about all this?"

"I'm not giving you the money," Trudy said.

"I see," Soldier said. "Spunk. Not much respect, but spunk. Just the same, I'm feeling generous as Jesus, so we'll do this Paco's way. We'll go to Leonard's . . . Leonard, that's the nigger, right?"

"Right," Paco said.

"We'll go to the nigger's place, dig up the money, take it and go our merry way, leave you holding your asses. How's that sound? You up for that, Howard? A little digging?"

There were tears on Howard's cheeks. "Yes," he said.

"Good," Soldier said. "Knowing you're happy makes me happy."

2 3

Soldier went through Chub's pockets, took his money and the mini-van keys. He put on the porkpie and got his umbrella. We left Chub where he lay and went out into the rain.

Soldier and Angel had a worn white Lincoln parked on the other side of the concession, and we went there first, stood in the cold rain while Soldier told us a little about respect. Paco got behind the wheel of the Lincoln. Angel sat up front, twisted in her seat to watch Howard and Trudy in the back.

They left ahead of us.

Soldier made me drive the mini-van. He put Leonard beside me, and he took the backseat. "Don't drive fast and don't think about any stupid shit like wrecking. I can put a bullet in both of you before we wrap around a telephone pole."

I didn't know which was preferable, a telephone pole or a bullet. I didn't want either.

I put the van in gear and started driving. When we were on the highway, Soldier tapped me on the shoulder with the automatic. "Angel. Whatda ya think of her? How she looks, I mean."

"She's all right," I said. "The gun takes away some."

"Those muscles bother you?"

"No."

"Yeah. Well, I tell you. Climb on top of her, it's like climbing on boulders. You can get a bruise. Stick your dick in her, you don't know you're getting it back. Got a bear trap for a pussy. We're talking about getting married. Whatda ya think?"

"You're a match made in heaven," I said.

"Yeah, maybe," he said. "But I don't know a man ought to marry some woman can bench press more than him, know what I'm saying? It far to the nigger's place?"

"Reasonably far," I said.

"Yeah, well, drive careful. I've seen some bad wrecks, weather like this."

By the time we got there the weather had really gotten bad. There were flakes of snow mixed in with the blowing rain and ice and the sky was dark as near sunset. Last time I had eaten was early that morning, and I was famished and felt a little light-headed.

We went into the house, which had been left unlocked, and Angel was standing by the couch holding her gun. Paco had his automatic in his waistband and he was stacking kindling in the fireplace. Trudy and Howard sat on the couch side by side with their hands on their knees. They glanced up when we came in, then glanced away.

Soldier shook out his umbrella on the living room floor and snapped it shut so briskly we all jumped. He smiled and propped the umbrella against the door frame.

Angel waved me and Leonard over to the couch, made us sit with Trudy and Howard. It was a tight fit. Me, Leonard, Trudy and Howard, the four dumb assholes.

Angel leaned on the wall next to the fireplace, held her gun against her thigh and watched us. Her eyes were dark and clueless.

"Look around," Soldier told Angel. "Paco, you watch things. I'm going to find the head." He went in search of the bathroom and Angel went out the back way.

Paco pulled the automatic out of his pants as if the act were tiring, stood by the couch and hardly looked at us at all.

I said softly to Paco, "Guess this is what you meant by a truck going downhill."

"Guess so," he said.

"You should have robbed the World Savers," Leonard said. "Fat boy would still be with us if you'd done that."

"I didn't want that to happen," Paco said. "But what happens happens. Soldier's got some possibilities for me. I'm willing to gamble for the bigger score. I robbed these fools I'd have that money and that's it."

"You could have set your own deals," I said.

"Soldier, he's got better connections. He's done some big deals."

"Drugs?" Leonard said.

"Drugs," Paco said.

"But the guy's crazy," I said. "He may have some connections, but he's not firing on all cylinders. He thinks he's some kind of gangster."

"He is . . . and he's fucked in the head. I don't like him any, but I've seen the kind of dough he gets. I invest my part here, I could make millions, then I'm out of the shit for good. I'll buy me a face and a life."

"You don't have to do this," I said.

"Think I don't know that?" Paco said. "I throw in with you, what do I get? Your gratitude? I can't buy a thing with that. Guy like me, record I got, way I look. This is the end of the line, and I'm going to throw the dice for the big one this one last time."

Soldier came back.

"Got a slow flush in there, nigger. Water pressure's down."

Angel came in the front door.

"How's things?" Soldier asked her.

She nodded.

Paco returned the automatic to the front of his pants and placed a couple of logs on the kindling and lit the pile with one of the big matches. It smoked a little, began to catch. "I'm going to light the heaters," he said, and he went about the house doing just that. When he came back into the room he returned to the fireplace and poked another log into the flames.

Soldier watched him, pushed his hat back on his head and let his right hand rest on the hilt of the automatic jammed into the front of his pants. His face still had that unhealthy sheen of sweat. He worked his tongue around inside his bottom lip and said, "You going to make some sandwiches next, Paco? Get cozy, maybe have a little picnic?"

Paco turned and said, "Look here, Soldier, don't give me a

hard time. I'm sick to death of being cold. And I ought to make a sandwich. We could all use a sandwich. None of us have eaten."

"You got to think about this kind of shit ahead of time. Me and Angel we ate, didn't we, Angel?"

Angel nodded.

"When was it, right at noon, when you're supposed to eat? Had some sandwiches. What was it we had, Angel?"

"Bologna."

"Yeah, bologna. Listen here, now, we get through with this little deal, I'll buy you a steak. Hey, I'll even buy these shits a steak. Okay? Hey, you, the dick, what is it? Harry?"

"Howard," Angel said.

"Come on, let's go do some digging," Soldier said. "Hell, all of you come. I'm going out in the shit, you're all going. We need a shovel for this?"

"Yes," Howard said. "It's in the barn."

"Maybe you and the girlie drew a little treasure map. Something with an *X* on it, you know. Says Dig Here. You do that, Howard, draw a little treasure map?"

"We dig up the money, you'll let us go?" Howard said.

Soldier spread his hands. "Hey, you don't show me the money, you got no luck. I see some money, I can get happy. Nice things might happen. Let's go."

We went out to the barn. The dogs barked at us as we went by their pens. "Tell 'em to shut up," Soldier said, "or I'll blow their fucking heads off. I hate dogs."

"Quiet," Leonard said. "Hush down."

The dogs softened their barks, and we went inside the barn through the side door. It was only slightly warmer inside than out. Soldier leaned on Trudy's Volkswagen and breathed out a cloud of vapor. "Up north they heat barns. Okay, whatcher name, what's the scoop on the money?"

"We buried it here in the barn," Howard said.

Soldier folded up his umbrella neatly and put it on top of Trudy's car. He said, "Didn't want to be cold while you were digging, that it? Get the shovel."

"It won't do any good," Trudy said.

"Yeah," Soldier said. "Tell you what, cunt. Shut up! Angel, she says another word, you fix her nose a little."

Angel nodded.

Howard got the shovel. He went around front of the Volkswagen and began to dig.

"Barns in the north," Soldier said, "they got floors. Maybe you niggers and white trash should go on and do it right. Forget the fucking walls too."

Howard stopped digging, got down on his hands and knees, moved his fingers in the dirt. He looked up at Soldier. "It's . . . not here."

I thought immediately of last night and Trudy's second walk, the clay and gravel on her pants and boots. She had moved the money somewhere near the creek. She may have hardened in her dedication, but her final trust of men hadn't changed. She was for damn sure the one on the steed now.

I looked at Trudy. She was staring straight ahead. Howard was looking up at her with eyes like a kicked puppy. She'd done it to him again.

"I see," Soldier said. He said to Angel, "It's gone, honey, whatda you think?"

Angel shrugged.

Soldier pulled his automatic out of his waistband, then put it back. He took off his hat and ran his hand through his hair. He put the hat back on and took a small packet of Kleenex out of his windbreaker pocket, carefully peeled it open, and pulled one out. He returned the packet to his pocket and used the Kleenex to clean his glasses. He put his glasses on again and dabbed his face with the Kleenex.

"Okay," he said. "The money isn't there." He tossed the used Kleenex on the ground. "Howard, give me the shovel."

Howard was still squatting by the hole, trying to sort things out. He used the shovel to help himself up, gave it to Soldier.

Soldier said, "Thanks, Howard. Stand over there, will you? About there." He looked at the hole, looked at Howard. "You're sure you dug deep enough?"

Howard nodded.

Soldier got a good grip on the shovel near the top of the handle and swung it around smoothly and caught Howard above the ear with the back of the shovel blade. Howard's head rang as if it were hollow. He fell out on his back and didn't move. Soldier put the blade of the shovel against Howard's neck, raised his foot to stomp it into him.

Trudy yelled, "Leave him alone! I took the money and hid it, you cretin! You rotten sonofabitch! Leave him alone!"

2 4

Soldier took the shovel from Howard's throat and flung it aside. It went by me, missing my head by about a foot.

"Goddammit, Paco," Soldier said. "You said this would be an easy score. Just wear our leotards, dance in and take the money. This hasn't been easy. This is boring. This is bullshit!"

"Trudy," Paco said. "Give us the money. We'll let you go if you do. There's no other way."

"You lying double-crossing shit," Trudy said.

"That's me," Paco said. "Now give us the money. It'll only be hard for you if you don't."

"It damn sure will," Soldier said.

"I'm talking here," Paco said. "You're not the only one's killed somebody, you know."

"Oh," Soldier said, "listen to you. The goddamn creature from hell, and now you're talking some orders. Don't you forget, freak. I'm the one gives the orders."

They stared at one another for a hard moment. Paco had his automatic in his fist and Soldier's was still in his pants. He had his hand resting on it.

"This is some shit, Paco," Soldier said. "You and me trying to showdown on one another. We're partners. Right, huh? Right?"

"Close enough," Paco said. His voice was firm but I could see his legs were vibrating slightly.

"Let's don't say some things we'll regret," Soldier said. "Let's go on to the house, talk a little. Trudy here, she'll see to reason. Won't you, Trudy?"

"I'm not telling you where the money is," Trudy said.

"All right," Soldier said. "You're not telling. Not now. Things can change, though. You, Happy Man. You and the nigger. Get what's his name, Howie, Howard, whatever the fuck. Carry him to the house."

We put Howard on the couch and Trudy and Paco took chairs and me and Leonard sat on the brick hearth before the fire. Angel stood in front of us with her gun. She seemed as natural as part of the furniture.

Soldier sat at the kitchen table and called out to us. "Maybe Paco's right. We all get a little something to eat, we'll feel better. More cooperative, you know. He awake?"

Angel went over to the couch and turned Howard's head with her hand. I could see a knot the size of an orange at the front of his ear and the middle of the knot was cut and oozing blood.

"No?" Soldier said. "Well, we can save him a little something for later. Paco, what say you make the sandwiches? Am I bossing again, huh?"

"I'll do it," Paco said.

He did. We had sandwiches made of leftover meatloaf. I don't really remember eating it, which, considering Leonard's meatloaf, is no loss, but I certainly needed it. I felt a small measure of strength return.

"Everybody eaten now?" Soldier said. "All right. We got that out of the way. We're all feeling less grumpy, am I right? Doody, come over here and see me."

"Trudy," Angel said.

"Trudy, then, whatever. Just get over here."

"I'm not telling you where the money is."

"Come here anyway. Angel, give her some help."

Angel pulled Trudy to her feet, pushed her toward the kitchen table. Trudy went over and sat in the chair across from Soldier.

Soldier smiled at her. "Not still hungry, are you? Need a glass of water? No. Good. Now listen here. What we got is a simple problem, but you're making it into one of those whatya call its . . . Angel, help me out here."

"Dilemmas."

"Yeah. One of them. It's really a lot more simple than that. You give me the money, and we go away. You don't give me the money, I shoot you. And all your friends too. The nigger and Happy. All of you end up like the fat boy back at the Apache. Brains on the wall. It's not a good way, Trudy."

"You're going to kill us anyway," Trudy said.

"No. No. I'm going to let you go. I'll take the money, get long gone, and hey, next day you're back to whatever you were doing before we came together here."

"I tell you where the money is, you'll kill us," Trudy said. "And if you're going to kill us anyway, I'm not going to tell you where it is. If I'm going to die, it's knowing you haven't got the money."

"That's tough, Trudy. You're a hard little cunt, I give you that. You seen a man's brains blown out and one get it with a shovel, and you're still talking to me like we got some negotiations here. Last time you and, what's his name, Howie, Henry . . . "

"Howard," Angel said.

"Yeah, him. Two of you didn't do so good, you know? I mean, you got no guns. You got nothing."

"And you don't have the money," Trudy said. "That money was for an idea, an important one—"

Soldier made a fiddling motion with his left arm and right hand. His lips drooped at the corners and pursed.

"—and you just want it to spend."

"You think all I want is to spend this money? Any fool can spend money. Buy a gallon of milk, a pound of butter, new economy car. Trip to Tahoe. Bullshit. There's spending, then there's spending. I'm a regular goddamned cona . . . What am I saying here, Angel?"

"Connoisseur."

"That. You see, baby, I've made more money in a day than you got hid out there. This bit of shit, four hundred thousand or so, that's nothing. But this is supposed to be an easy score, see, and you're making it not so easy, and I'm getting hardheaded about it.

It's the principle of the thing now. How do you think I'm going to feel about myself I let this go? I said I was going to get the money, and I'm going to get the money. Takes a little time, it takes a little time. But if it takes time, it's going to seem a hell of a lot longer to you, Doody. Hear me? And in the end, no matter what, I'm going to get the money."

"Not if I don't tell you," Trudy said.

"You'll tell me. Look, here's what I'll do. To show I'm no hard guy." He pulled out the five thousand Howard had given him and put it on the table. "I give this back. Yours. Not to split with anyone else. All yours. Buy you a little something nice, new dress. Get your hair done. Whatever. Your money. All you got to do is tell me where the main pile is. You give me the big wad, I let you and everyone else go. The nigger too. And you make a little change. And I tell you, I'm in a good mood when I get the money, I might toss in a little bonus for everybody. Whatda you say? We got a deal?"

"Go fuck yourself."

Soldier's sweaty face went red. "Have it your way."

He got up and walked around the table. Put his hands on the back of Trudy's chair, bent so that his chin touched the top of her head. My muscles bunched in the center of my back like a knot being tied.

"You're sure?" he said.

"I'm as sure as I've ever been," Trudy said.

Soldier straightened up, looked around the kitchen. He went over to the cabinet Leonard was building and got the hammer, took one of the long nails from the paper bag. He went back to his chair at the table, said, "Angel. Can you come over here a moment? I'm going to need your help."

"Soldier," Paco said. "Don't."

"Paco," Soldier said, "I've let you fuck with me a lot. Don't think my good humor's going to hold out forever. There's money and I want it. You want it, don't you? Want what I can do for you?"

Paco paused.

"Well?" Soldier said.

"Yeah," Paco said, and he was barely audible.

"Then," Soldier said, "we've got to get this show on the road." He took off his hat and tossed it in the corner. "Angel, take hold of her left hand."

25

I had only thought I had been helpless before. I could see what was coming and I wanted to stop it, wanted to do something heroic like leap over the couch and go for Soldier and break his neck. I had the ability to break his neck, but I had no reason to believe I could reach him. Paco might not want things to be like they were, but he had cast his lot, and would shoot me before I had gone six feet. And if he didn't, there was Angel. She had her gun in the waist of her jogging pants, but she was far enough away she could draw and fire. And then there was Soldier.

If I died, that left Leonard and Howard and Trudy against this bunch, and Trudy wasn't going to be worth much in a moment. Howard was out of it. I had to bide my time.

I could tell them I knew the money was along the creek, but even so, I didn't know where. Bottom line was I couldn't lead them straight to it, and I couldn't depend on luck. And even if they got the money, Trudy was right. Soldier was going to kill us.

"Open your hand and put it on the table," Soldier told Trudy.

Trudy didn't move. She sat with her hands in her lap staring straight ahead.

Angel took hold of Trudy's hand. Trudy made a fist. Angel slapped her. Trudy let out a cry. Angel opened Trudy's hand with both of hers and pushed it flat against the table, palm down, and held her by the wrist.

"Do it, you pig," Trudy said. "Do it!"

Soldier put the nail against the back of Trudy's hand and the hammer came down quick and the nail went through and Trudy screamed and the table rocked. Her fingers thrashed like heated caterpillars.

Angel let go of Trudy's hand and stepped back from the table. She turned to look out the kitchen window, as if distracted by a bird.

"Now," Soldier said. "The money. Or the other hand."

Trudy opened her mouth, but nothing came out.

"That's all right," Soldier said. "Rest a little. You'll get your voice back. But you don't tell me about that money, it's the other hand. That don't work, we got to do a tit."

I had stood up when the hammer came down, but there was nowhere to go and nothing to do that wouldn't get me killed.

"Sit down," Paco said.

I sat down. I felt small in my clothes. I could see the side of Trudy's face. Her eyelid was fluttering rapidly. Soldier said, "That had been me, I think I'd have passed out. You got balls on you, sister. I give you that. But hey, this has got to hurt. Am I right? Let's stop this unpleasantness. I want you to stop being obstrap, ob . . . What am I going for here, Angel?"

"Obstreperous."

"There you go. Obstreperous. Where's the money?"

Trudy's voice was a rasp, but the words were clear. "Eat shit."

Soldier leaned over the table and slapped her. She fell back out of the chair and the table turned over and the edge of it hit her in the neck. The fall stretched her hand to the limit the nail would allow. She lay there and made little sobbing noises while the five thousand dollars fluttered all over like a shattered head of lettuce.

In that instant I wanted her to tell what she knew. Let them have the money and shoot us, get it over with, and in that same instant my survival instincts rose up in me and I knew I had maybe one card to play, and I had to play it now or fold and count the lot of us out.

"I know where the money is," I said.

"What?" Soldier said. "You, Happy Guy. What's that?"

"I know where the money is."

"He's lying," Paco said. "He never left this house. He wouldn't know where she buried it. If he did, he wouldn't have let her go through with this. He's stalling."

Leonard was watching Paco like a dog watched a favorite bone. All right, Paco was Leonard's. I'd count on that.

That left Angel and Soldier.

"It just came to me where it is," I said. "I remember when she came in, what she had on her shoes."

"Shoes?" Soldier said. "We're talking shoes? I'm talking money, I don't know from shoes, Mr. Happy. Money, the moola, the green."

"I know where the money is because of her shoes."

"I see," Soldier said. "One of those clue things, huh?"

"Something like that," I said. "Give me a shovel, and I'll give you the money."

"Hey, there we are," Soldier said. "Angel. He's going to give us the money. Hear that?"

Angel nodded.

"You're all right, Happy. I could get to like you."

"I don't want to like you," I said. "I want to get this over with. I give you the money, and you let us go."

"Have I ever said different?" Soldier said. "This's the deal I been trying to shake all day. Give me the money, I let you go. That's what I been saying, right? That's right, isn't it Angel?"

"That's right," Angel said.

"Let's go, Happy," Soldier said, "you and me."

"All of us," I said.

"All of us?" Soldier said. "You're telling me, all of us? Everybody's a boss here. I mean, I'm supposed to be the boss, and I got no say."

"I want Trudy doctored," I said. "I want her with us. I don't want to leave her with Angel. Angel likes what she does too much."

"We'll leave her with Paco."

"No."

"Now you're trying to negotiate. You see where this gets you. A nail in the hand. Lying on the floor."

"My way, in twenty, thirty minutes, you'll have the money," I said. "Your way could go on all day."

"If you're tough as she is," Soldier said.

"I don't think I am," I said. "But I might be tough enough to last for a while. Longer than twenty or thirty minutes."

The sweat on Soldier's face looked like a thick coating of Vaseline. He wrinkled his brows and nodded.

"You got a point on the time thing, Happy Man. Not a good one, but a point. But hey, I'm sick of dicking around. I want to . . . What is it when you want to speed things up, Angel?"

"Expedite."

"Expedite. That'll do. So, deal."

Soldier squatted behind the over-turned table, took the hammer, and hit the point of the nail hard. Trudy let out a yelp and bent at the waist and almost sat up before falling back down. The head of the big nail poked out of the back of her hand, but it was still partially in the table.

Angel got hold of Trudy's wrist, jerked hard and the nail came out of the table and the head of it caught on the back of Trudy's hand. Angel grabbed the nail from the bottom and shoved it through most of the way, then caught the head of it between two fingers, yanked it free and tossed it on the floor. She let go of Trudy's wrist and put the overturned chair upright and sat Trudy in it. Trudy was as white as plaster.

"Get the monkey blood, tie a rag around her hand, whatever you want," Soldier said. "Let's get this over with."

2 6

Angel brought some alcohol from Leonard's medicine cabinet, tore up a pillowcase, and let me dress Trudy's hand at the kitchen sink. Trudy was still white and a little wobbly and she flinched when I poured the alcohol on her hand, but not much. After being nailed to a table, alcohol was a treat.

"I'm sorry," I said.

"I made my own choices," she said. "You don't know where the money is, do you, Hap?"

I didn't answer.

"If you do, don't tell them. They're going to kill us anyway. Let's don't give them the satisfaction of the money. Scum like this, they'll buy drugs, sell them to kids if they can make a dime."

"Hey," Soldier said. "Quit the debate. Happy Man's giving me the money. And I tell you, it's not so bad a kid or two's got some dope, way things are. Little dope's better than some things. Let's roll."

I wrapped the strips of pillowcase tight around her hand. Blood spotted through it in a matter of seconds, but it was the best I could do.

"Everybody out into the great outdoors," Soldier said. He went over to the couch to prod Howard with the barrel of his automatic, but Howard didn't move. Soldier bent and put his head to Howard's chest. "This one's checked out. Shit, I hit guys harder than that before and they didn't die."

"You sonofabitch," Trudy said. "You sorry sonofabitch."

"You hadn't dug up the money and moved it on old Howard, he'd be with us today," Soldier said. "But no, you got to be the smart bitch. Then you got to get a nail through your hand for nothing, 'cause old Happy Man here is going to lead me to the dough anyway."

"He doesn't know where it is," Trudy said.

"Yes, I do," I said. "I figured it out."

"You better have," Soldier said, "or it's going to sound like the Fourth of July around here for about a minute. Let's go."

Soldier got his umbrella and put his hat on. I put an arm around Trudy, and Soldier waved Leonard in close to us and the three of us led out, Paco, Angel, and Soldier close behind.

Outside, the blowing rain and sleet had stopped, but it was cold and wet and there was the sound of thunder. I bent over and kissed Trudy next to her ear, whispered, "Just follow my lead."

"No talking," Soldier said. "You get to talking, I get nervous. I like to do the talking."

I walked straight to the barn. When we were inside, I let go of Trudy and she wobbled, but Leonard stepped in and held her up. I went over and got the shovel where Soldier had tossed it.

I started outside again.

"It's not in here?" Soldier said. "We got to go back out in that shit?"

I didn't say anything. I went out and Leonard followed, helping Trudy. The armed trio followed us.

I went straight to Switch's pen, and when Leonard saw where I was going, he picked up his speed slightly. I stopped in front of the pen, and Switch came out of his house and walked cautiously toward me.

"You all right now?" Leonard said to Trudy.

"I'm all right," she said. "I can stand just fine."

Leonard let go of her and came over to the dog pen and said, "Switch, ol' buddy."

Switch came over and Leonard looked at me out of the corner of his eye. I knew then he understood what I was up to.

"What's with stopping to pet the mutt?" Soldier said. "You on vacation here?"

"The money's here," I said. "One of these pens. I don't know which one, but one. When she came back that night, the second time, she had dog shit on her shoes. This is the most likely place for her to get it. I think she buried it in one of these pens."

"Think?" Soldier said.

"You can just about count on it," I said.

"You got to count on it," Soldier said. "Paco, what you think?"

"Could be," Paco said. "Probably is."

"Angel?" Soldier said.

Angel shrugged.

"What am I asking you for?" Soldier said. "You got your three squares, one of those protein milkshakes, some barbells, you're happy, aren't you?"

Angel's expression didn't change.

"You could be one of those things," Soldier said. "What is it I'm trying to say here, Angel? Like a robot kind of."

"Android," she said.

"Yeah, one of them. You know, sometimes you give me the willies."

I opened the dog pen and reached in and got hold of Switch's collar and said, "Good dog." I pulled him out. I could feel his muscles bunching at the smell of all these strangers.

"Whatda you doing?" Soldier said.

"Getting him out of the way so I can dig," I said. "Leonard, hold him."

Leonard reached over and held him and took a step backwards and pulled the dog after him, stuck out his free hand and touched Soldier's shoulder and said, "Ow!"

It was all Switch needed, thinking Leonard was hurt. He twisted in Leonard's grip and Leonard let go and Switch leapt straight into Soldier and Soldier dropped his umbrella and threw up his arm. The dog had him hard as a mallet, teeth flashing.

I had already started toward the group with the shovel cocked, and when Switch hit Soldier and Soldier yelled, Angel and Paco turned their heads, and I brought the shovel around with all my might and caught Angel on the side of the neck with the edge of it and it was like hitting a concrete piling. She went down on one knee and her gun arm dropped to her side and her neck split open and lashed a band of blood into the cold air and rain.

Leonard stepped behind Soldier and the dog, pivoted on his left foot and spun around, fast, and his right leg went up, and at the same instant Paco raised his gun and leveled it, Leonard's foot caught him in the back of the head, low, and Paco snapped forward and the gun went off but didn't hit anyone. Next instant Paco was face down on the ground with his butt humping like a worm trying to crawl.

Leonard's heel kick had broken Paco's neck.

Switch had Soldier down and his teeth buried in Soldier's arm. He was dragging him backwards on the muddy ground, gnawing as he went, tearing jacket and shirt and meat beneath.

I brought the shovel around again and hit Angel solidly on top of her head and she dropped her gun and went down on her hands as if to do a push-up. I started to go for her gun but Soldier managed to put his automatic to Switch's head and pull the trigger. Switch jerked, then was on the ground thrashing. Soldier was getting up on one knee now, his hat was gone and his glasses dangled from one ear.

He gritted his teeth, lifted the .45, and pointed it at Trudy.

Trudy hadn't moved through all of this, but I was moving. I grabbed her around the waist, jerked her to the side and the bullet went by us. As I turned, I saw Leonard sprint behind the dog pens toward the creek and saw Angel scramble for her gun. I got hold of Trudy like she was a sack of potatoes and ran zigzag toward the creek.

Trudy was too much for me and I dropped her. There was a sudden sensation as if someone punched me in the right side with the end of a fence post. I went down on one knee and yelled, "Run!" Then I was up again, and Trudy was already moving, long legs flying. She went over the creekbank and into the water just ahead of me. There was another snap of gunfire, then I was in the creek right behind Trudy, splashing water, running for all I was worth. The brush on the sides of the bank grew thicker as we headed into the greater woods.

Back toward the house I heard several shots and a dog yelp and Soldier yelling. I was surprised they weren't on us right away, and wondered if they had gone after Leonard.

As I ran, pain crawled inside me looking for a place to live.

I felt as if my very soul were easing out of me, falling into the water, washing away.

But when I looked down, I saw what was oozing out of me into the water was not my soul.

It was blood.

27

I wasn't exactly making the best time in the world, and Trudy wasn't much of a runner to begin with. I could hear Angel and Soldier thrashing through the water behind us. They sounded some distance back, but they were gaining rapidly. Angel had the constitution of a horse and a head like an iron skillet. Soldier had popped poor old Howard half as hard and only once, and he hadn't survived.

I caught up with Trudy and grabbed her by the elbow and pointed to the bank. We climbed out of the water and crawled into a mess of leafless brambles and through that and into a grove of pines and sweetgums.

We hadn't gone far, when I had to sit down. I found a sweetgum and put my back against that and eased myself to my ass. Trudy, breathing heavily, squatted beside me and looked at my side. My coat was bloody and I could feel the blood cooling and sticking my shirt to my skin.

"Oh, Hap," Trudy said.

I put a finger to my lips. I could hear Soldier and Angel splashing water in the creek. They went past us and kept splashing.

When I thought they were reasonable out of the way, I spoke softly. "Your hand. How is it?"

"Numb," she said. "Mostly it's shock. But that's passing some.

All things considered, I'm all right."

"Well, I'm not. Help me up."

She got her good hand under my arm and I pushed up and leaned on her a minute. "We got to make the Robin Hood Tree."

"What?"

"Trust me."

It wasn't far from where we were, but it felt like a mile. My side had little feeling in it at first, but now it was as if someone had heated up a jack handle and was sticking it into me, stirring it around.

We went through deeper woods and promptly broke into a clearing, and there in its center was the massive oak that Leonard and I called the Robin Hood Tree. Sitting down, his back against it, was Leonard.

We walked up to him and he opened his eyes and looked at us. "If you'd been Angel or that other geek, I'd be dead."

"You're hit?"

"Caught me in the back, low, to the right. Came out the side of my leg here." He touched his right thigh gently. "Bone turned the slug, I guess. It was Angel shot me. Bitch is good. I was well on the run, ahead of you two, going into the woods along the creek. Thought I had it made."

I squatted down beside him, wiped cold sweat off his forehead with my fingers, rubbed it on my pants. "It'll be all right, Leonard."

"Damn right it will," he said. "I been worse . . . Shit, man, you're hit too."

"High in the side, came out the front here," I said. "I'm scared to look, but—"

"You been worse," Leonard said.

"Right."

"Trudy," Leonard said, "you've had yourself quite a time playing revolutionary, haven't you?"

"I believe what I believe," she said. "None of this changes anything."

"This," Leonard said, "isn't over. But I got to hand it to you, had it been me and Soldier had brought out that hammer, I'd have sang like a parakeet."

A freezing rain came slanting through the trees from the

north and hit the clearing, then the oak and us.

"We stay here, we'll freeze," I said.

"Can't we go through the woods?" Trudy said. "It's got to stop somewhere."

"It stops, all right," I said. "Several miles later. As cold and close to dark as it is, I don't think me and Leonard could make it with these wounds."

"Trudy maybe could make it," Leonard said. "Get some help."

"I don't know the woods," Trudy said. "I'd be going in circles before I was out of sight of this tree."

"Doubt we'd survive till you got back anyway," I said. "If Soldier and Angel didn't find us, we'd most likely freeze or bleed to death. We can go wide to the main road, or back to the house. Chance Soldier and Angel being gone right now. Get Leonard's car and haul out."

"It's got to be that for me," Leonard said. "I go too far in any direction, maybe even back to the house, and I'll be growing grass over me come spring."

"We might wait them out," Trudy said.

"We'd be icicles first," Leonard said. "And besides, I got a rifle in the trunk of the car, a target pistol in the house. They could be some insurance."

"Then it's settled," I said.

"Hap, break me off a limb," Leonard said. "Got to have a crutch."

I had to go easy, but I walked until I came to a sweetgum at the edge of the clearing, got hold of a two-inch limb and pulled on it. I felt as if my guts were being wrenched out, but I kept at it until I heard it crack, then I swung on it until I got it so I could twist it off. It had a couple of whispy limbs on it, and I managed to break those off underfoot. It wasn't going to make a comfortable crutch, but by hooking it in the crook of his arm, it might do. It had a kind of point on the end too, where I had twisted it off, and I thought that would be good, something he could push into the ground.

Trudy helped me get Leonard up. He got the stick positioned and tried it and it worked well enough.

"Don't wait on me," he said. "One of us has got to get back to the house and the car, get some help."

"It's all or nothing," Trudy said.

2 8

We eased forward, wide of the creek, broke through the woods and out into the clearing where the house was visible through the ever-thickening slants of icy rain. To make matters worse, the wind had picked up and was driving the rain against us as if it were frozen needles. I felt feverish, and as if something important had broken inside me. Everything was a little surreal. I was still losing blood.

We huddled together, me and Trudy on either side of Leonard, helping him along. He looked like something for a pine box and six feet of dirt.

I thought about Soldier and Angel, realized that if they had come back by the creek, they could already be at the house, waiting. But if we could get to the car and get it started . . . That was thinking too far ahead.

Keep walking. One foot in front of the other and this fever is the heat of the sun and it's mid-July and the fish are biting and the grass is going brown and the trees are wilting like overworked washerwomen. Yes sir, it's not cold, it's hot, it's hot, gimmea left. Left. Adaleft, left, left, adaleft, left, had a good home but I left, left. Hell, maybe I shouldn't have fought the draft. I had the march down. Then I realized I was talking out loud, and I shut up and zeroed in on the dog pens and made for them, tried not to think about Soldier and Angel or that they might be waiting for us to come into range so they could spray the place with our brains. It would be quicker and better than dying slowly in the woods from the wet cold.

Next thing I knew we were at the dog pens, and I understood why we had gotten as much of a head start on them as we had, saw what all that shooting we heard was about. Leonard's dogs. In his fury, Soldier had killed them all.

"That motherfucker," Leonard said. "I ever get the chance, half the chance, he's a dead cocksucker. Dead."

Paco lay where we had left him. He was face down, on his knees, his head bent under him, as if folded. That had been some kick. His false teeth lay over in the mud near Soldier's open umbrella, mashed porkpie and the shovel. Trudy turned Paco over to see if his gun was still under him, but Soldier, though stupid, wasn't that stupid.

"I wasn't on this stick," Leonard said, "I'd go over and kick that fucker till he came back to life."

"Go straight for your car," I said.

We did. The car was parked at the side of the house, near the front porch, where it had been left when brought out by the Ice Birds, as Leonard called them.

Leonard worked the keys out of his pants pocket and Trudy opened the car door and Leonard slid in and tried to start it. Nothing. It didn't even click.

I went around and opened the hood. Doing it made me feel as if my intestines were falling out of me, but when I looked inside, I knew our problem wasn't the weather, and I understood Soldier's and Angel's delay in pursuing us even better. They had taken the distributor cap. I limped over to the mini-van and looked under its hood. Same thing. And the Lincoln. And the Volvo. I thought about checking the Volkswagen in the barn, but I couldn't believe they'd leave it undone, not after taking time for the others. Besides, I didn't feel as if I could make it to the barn.

"The rifle," Leonard said.

I got his keys and limped around there with Trudy, and was about to unlock the trunk, when there was a crack and the back glass of Leonard's car exploded into jagged stars. I saw Soldier and Angel coming up over the bank. They were covered in mud from the feet to the knees. Their faces were red and limb-whipped. Not happy campers. They were still a good distance away and not moving at top speed due to the cold blasting rain, but those guns gave them a lot of reach.

I whirled to run and there was another shot, and Trudy, who was slightly in front of me, threw out her hands and went face down. I grabbed her by the coat collar and started yelling for Leonard and there was another shot, small caliber, the .38. Then I was dragging Trudy toward the front porch of the house, my wound making my insides jump hard against my bones, and Leonard was limping behind. I heard him let out a grunt and I glanced back and saw him go down on one knee and saw blood flowing out of him to be washed across the cold ground in a dark wave; saw too that Soldier and Angel were coming on hard and fast.

Leonard scrambled for his stick and screamed himself up and yelled something at me that the pounding rain took away, and then I had Trudy pulled up on the porch and my shoulder took a bullet and I grunted and opened the door and hauled her halfway inside and staggered back for Leonard.

He almost ran over me before I could get off the porch. He let out a yell and I felt a punch in my chest and I grabbed him and swung him through the door and he and his stick went sliding across the floor. I fast-limped in, got hold of Trudy and pulled her all the way inside and slammed the door and locked it and Soldier hit it with his body and yelled. I thought Angel would hit it next, take it off its hinges, but that didn't happen. There was silence. And that was more frightening than the noise. I made my way across the room and into the kitchen, to the back door. I locked it just before the knob began to rattle and Soldier began to cuss. He fired two shots, quick succession, through the door about head high. I was just enough out of the way and the slugs slammed into the wall and picked a crock pot off a shelf and sent pieces of it all over.

I stumbled toward the living room, and as I passed the kitchen window, two more shots punched at the glass and threw up the curtains and slammed into the wall, but I was out of there and into the living room.

I avoided the window in the living room by getting low. I went over to Leonard. He was on the floor. Blood was running out of his leg and just below his ribs. That would be the shot that hit him on the porch and went through and got me too, but not bad. Leonard had taken most of that one. The ones in my right side and shoulder, those were the sonofabitches. The one in my lower right chest was just picking at me.

Leonard had taken off his jacket and pulled off his shirt and was tying it around his leg, trying to stop the blood from pumping out. He had never lost his stick, and took hold of it again, tight.

Soldier was at the side of the house yelling. "Come on out, it's all over. Bam. A bullet in the head. You don't come out, I'm going to take some time with you."

I crawled around in front of the couch where poor dead Howard lay, and got a look at Trudy. The front of her jacket was a dark wet explosion where the bullet had come out. Viscera poked through the hole in the jacket. My face explained things to Leonard.

"I'm sorry," he said. "Not a thing you can do."

I tried using my hand to close her eyes but I couldn't get her lids to go down. It seemed very important that her eyes close so I wouldn't have to look at them, but the lids just wouldn't do it.

Two shots whizzed through the living room window and struck the fireplace mantel and ricocheted into something I couldn't identify. Arctic rain came through and hit my face and mixed with the tears on my cheeks. I found it almost pleasant.

"You with me, Hap?" Leonard said.

"Yeah," I said, but I wasn't so sure. It was as if my center of gravity had shifted.

"One time," Soldier yelled, "I caught me this nigger trying to do me on a drug deal. I took him out and nailed his balls to a stump and left him there. With a sharp knife. Hear me in there, nigger?"

"Just a couple of licks on him with this," Leonard said, shaking the stick. "That's all I ask."

"The target pistol?" I said.

"In the nightstand by the bed. Not loaded. Shells are there in a box . . . Hell, Hap. I got it bad."

"Hang on, buddy."

Soldier was quiet out there. Not a good sign.

"Look here, now," I said. "I'm going to get the pistol. You been worse, right?"

"Oh yeah."

To keep away from stray bullets, I crawled behind the couch and through the open door to the bedroom. I went like that until I was almost to the nightstand, but I never made it. I stopped crawling when I reached a pair of jogging shoes. With Angel's feet in them.

2 9

I looked up and there was her snubnose .38 and above it her impassive face with the right side and top of her forehead swollen all out of proportion from my shovel blows. One eye was almost closed. She looked like a Neanderthal. Behind her the bedroom window was up and the curtains flapped in the freezing wind above the bed and there were muddy footprints on the sheets.

She pulled the trigger on the .38.

It was empty.

She knew that.

Bitch.

She whipped her hand around and struck me on the side of the head with the gun, tossed it away, grabbed me by the coat and pulled me up. A network of pain went through my wounds and some new connection were found.

She kneed me in the nuts, tossed me backwards with a yell.

I hurtled through the open door and fell on my side in the living room behind the couch. Outside, I heard Soldier yell. "Angel? Angel?"

I rolled and tried to get up, but she got me by the collar and picked me up and tossed me over the couch. I rolled on my back and she leaned over the couch and grabbed Howard by his coat and crotch, and more shoved than threw him at me. He landed on his stomach across my legs.

She started around the couch making deep strides and I kicked out from under Howard and got unsteadily to my feet.

"Watch her, watch her," Leonard yelled, as if I might decide to go take in a little TV. When she came around the couch, she kicked at Leonard, who was doing his damnedest to get up, caught him a glancing blow on the head. But he wasn't her main target. He seemed for the most part incapacitated. And she hadn't forgotten me and that shovel.

She reached for me and I shot out a left jab and her head went back and her nose broke open and spouted blood. I hit her again, and again. Good jabs.

She stepped in and grabbed me and whipped me up and around and I fell back on the couch. She came down on top of me and I squirmed out from under her, caught her under the arm and twisted her on her back, straddled her and hit her with a hard left-right combination. Her face was nothing but blood now.

She slammed her forearms into my sides, sending tentacles of pain into my side wound. I fell back on the floor, trying but unable to scream. Next thing I knew she was on top of me, slamming me in the face with her fists. I couldn't think, couldn't get oriented, couldn't fight back.

Then something long and dark and sharp came into view and it pushed back Angel's head and blood ran onto my face.

Leonard had rolled across the floor and shoved the broken end of his stick into her right eye.

She stood up stiffly. The stick stuck out of her face a full four feet, but it was firm in her head. She didn't take hold of it. She managed to step over me and start toward the fireplace, but got her feet tangled in Howard's legs and went face down. Most of her body landed on the couch, but her head missed and the stick in her eye hit the floor and the back of her head cocked up slightly but sharply, stayed that way.

Then there was a thrashing at the living room window. Soldier had the shovel and was using it to knock out what was left of the glass. Before I could get up, the shovel pulled out, and he kicked out the frame, stooped, and stepped inside, the .45 in front of him. Leonard, still lying on the floor, reached out and caught Soldier's ankle before his foot was firmly planted, sent him stumbling forward, but he got his feet under him again and went past Leonard and caught his foot on Trudy's outstretched arm and fell all the way this time, and when he hit I rolled and fought the explosions in my body and chopped down on his wrist with the edge of my hand. His fingers popped wide like a startled starfish, and the gun went sliding, and he crawled for it, but I got him around the neck and tried to choke him. He made it up to his knees and I went up on my knees too, and I tightened my forearm around his throat and tried to squeeze the life out of him. He pulled a knife from his pocket and flicked it open one-handed and brought it up and slashed me at the crook of my elbow, but I didn't let go, so he did it again, and this time I did.

I scuttled toward the living room window on my hands and knees, saw Leonard lying there, finally too much out of blood to move, and then I twisted and got up on one knee and Soldier was there, slashing at my face. I caught the blade in my hand and the slash went deep in my thumb and scraped on bone. I tried to get my legs under me and get up, but something had finally gone really bad inside me, and I couldn't.

Soldier jerked the blade back and cut me again that way, but I didn't feel it right then, and I dove forward and put my head between his legs and grabbed him behind the knees and popped my head up and caught him in the balls with the back of it and snatched his legs out from under him. His head hit the floor hard. Real hard. I crawled on top of him and got hold of his knife hand with my good left hand, twisted his thumb back and made him let go.

I picked up the knife and put it to his throat. All I had to do was thrust and rip. Hadn't this goddamned out-of-state racist asshole tried to kill me?

He looked at me through those pathetic glasses and I thought of this gawky, sweaty-faced bastard as a kid with a father who slapped his ear into a cauliflower and had convinced him it was for his own good and that dear old kid-beating, wife-beating dad was a good man that demanded respect. And in that same fleeting instant I remembered that I had not gone to war because I didn't want to kill needlessly for a cause I didn't believe in. And here we didn't even have a cause. Just a sad fuck-up without any hope.

I got off of him and held the knife close and said, "Roll on your stomach, Soldier, or I'll kill you."

"Easy," he said. "I got a bad dog bite here."

He rolled on his stomach. I cut his coat from the collar to the center of his back, then pulled the sleeves down so they caught at his elbows. I cut strips from his pants legs and tied his wrists. I cut the back of his pants open so I could pull them down around his knees. I took off his tennis shoes and used his shoestrings to tie his ankles. I rolled his socks up tight, lifted his head, and forced them in his mouth, just in case he might want to talk. I'd heard all of him I ever wanted to hear.

Leonard was trying to sit up. I closed the knife and put it in my pocked and helped him to a sitting position so he could lean against the front door.

"You should have killed him," Leonard said.

"I know."

"It's going to complicate things."

"I know."

"Same ole Hap."

I made a concentrated effort to rise, and had to use the edge of the couch for support, but I made it. Falling down only twice, I got to the place where the phone ought to have been, saw that it had been pulled out of the wall and tossed on the floor near the kitchen table. Soldier or Angel in their haste had made an effort to disable it, way they had the cars. I grunted and cussed on over there, took hold of it, held my heart in my mouth while I examined it. The little connection at the end of the wire was cracked from being ripped out of the wall and the phone had been thrown down hard enough to knock the back off and let the guts out, but the guts themselves appeared to be intact. Looked to me they had been in too big a hurry to do the job right. I hoped.

I shoved the phone's insides back into place and crawled over to the wall connection and snapped the clip into place and tried to hold my mouth just right while I punched 0. The operator came on the line after three rings and I had her connect me to the sheriff's office. I told them what I thought they ought to know and hung up. The phone was slick with the blood from my cut hand.

I crawled back to the door and sat up next to Leonard.

"We better come up with some story," Leonard said.

I thought awhile. I put my mouth to his ear so Soldier couldn't hear.

"That's for shit," he said.

"Got one better?"

He shook his head. "Hap, you know I told you I been worse?"

"Yeah."

"I lied."

"Me too," I said.

"We gonna make it?"

"I am," I said.

Leonard tried to laugh, but it hurt too much. He opened his hand. I took it and held it.

3 0

I remember coming awake on the way to the hospital in the ambulance, and there being a man from the sheriff's office there. He was determined to have some kind of statement. I think I gave him one. After that, things got hazy, then things got white and there was this light and people bending over me, then I was out again. When I awoke it was to sunlight shining through a hospital window.

A nurse came in and spoke to me and gave me some water and sat me up in bed so I could see out the window better, and later on she came back with an orderly and a wheelchair and they got me in that and pushed me over by the window for an even better look.

I sat and looked out on the hospital lawn. The bad, wet weather was gone and the sun was out and the trees on the big lawn were moving gently in the wind. It was probably a cold wind, but certainly nothing like the way things had been. I wanted to take that as some sort of sign of good things to come, but it wasn't long after that the doctor came in and he had a big man with him in a long black coat and another big man dressed up in hat and boots and the standard issue that the sheriff's office gives out.

The doctor was a little man with a bland face and thinning blond hair. He stood with his hands in front of him, left palm over right. He made me think of a preacher, way he stood there. He was very polite. He said, "Mr. Collins, I'm Dr. Dumas. You know, you been out three days."

"Three days?"

"That's right. And I got to tell you, you're a lucky man."

"I don't feel so lucky," I said.

The man from the sheriff's office took off his cowboy hat and showed me a vein-riddled bald head. He went over to the corner and leaned there. The big man in the long coat took the single chair and pulled it around so that he was straddling it. Both he and the sheriff's man had their eyes on me.

"You're lucky nonetheless. Fraction of an inch here, a fraction there, it could have made quite a difference. One bullet went in your back, just above your buttocks, about here, but it caught the fatty part and turned and came out on the right side in front of your hipbone. One in your shoulder tore some muscles, but punched on through. There was a slug lodged just under your skin, right below your sternum, slightly to the right. You weren't too bad to patch up."

"What about Leonard?" I said.

"Medical science has something to do with Mr. Pine's survival, but his constitution may be more amazing than even yours. But he won't be up and around as soon as you are. He's got some nasty internal injuries, and his leg, well, I don't know. He'll keep it, but he may not walk well on it."

"My compliments to you, Dr. Dumas."

"That's my job. These men are here to ask you a few questions," Dr. Dumas said. "I'll let them introduce themselves."

Dr. Dumas went out.

The man in the long coat said, "I'm Jack Divit." The man from the sheriff's office didn't introduce himself. He looked around the room like he was bored.

Divit said, "I'm with the FBI. Sheriff's office has a statement from you, and now that you're feeling better, we'd like one too. You don't mind going through it again, do you?"

I took a shallow breath and started telling it the way Leonard and I agreed to tell it.

"My ex-wife. Trudy Fawst. She came around and said she had a job for me and Leonard. She wanted us to recover a boat for her and some other people and if we did they'd pay us some money."

"They tell you why they wanted to recover the boat?"

"No. It didn't matter. It was a job. We recovered the boat and it had lots of money in it in watertight cannisters. They didn't want to pay us then and they took us with them, said they'd let us go later. Turned out they were going to use the money to buy guns so they could be revolutionaries, you know. Silly idea. One of their bunch, guy named Paco, was out to make his own score and he hooked them up with a guy named Soldier, woman named Angel. There weren't any guns and Trudy didn't bring the money along, except for five thousand dollars. She said the rest was at Leonard's and we ended up going back there, only there wasn't any money and things got out of hand."

"What about this money?" the man from the sheriff's department said. "You say you saw some money, then there wasn't but the five thousand."

"I don't know. There looked to be more than five thousand. I wasn't counting. If there was more, I don't know what happened to it."

"This guy, Soldier," Divit said. "He tells a different story."

"Does he? How is old Soldier?"

"Physically, pretty good," Divit said. "But you see, he's a boy we been wanting to see for a long time. He's got a record."

"Imagine that."

"He's got some bad things to his credit. Drugs. Arms. Murder. Rape. Been busy. This Angel that was with him, she wasn't exactly for the church choir either. But still, Soldier tells it different. He says there's some money. Says it was some kind of holdup money this Howard fella knew about. Says you were all trying to score."

"I told you what I know," I said. "I don't know where the money came from originally or what they did with it. Howard claimed it was buried on Leonard's place, but Trudy, before she died, told me different."

"She told you where it was?" Divit said.

"Nope. She said it wasn't on Leonard's place. That was just a lie she told Soldier to stall. You'd seen this guy in action, you'd have lied to him too if you thought it would save you. He's a real animal. But the bottom line is she told me it was gone forever."

"What do you think she meant by that, Mr. Collins?"

"I got the impression she was trying to tell me it was destroyed. She might have been out of her head then. She'd had a nail driven through her hand, lots of shock, you know."

"Yeah," Divit said. "That shock's bad stuff. But what Soldier says, it matches some facts. And this Paco guy, he turns out to be a big-time revolutionary, head of the Mechanics. We thought he was dead since way back."

"Yeah?"

"Yeah. And Soldier says this Paco told him this money was from a bank robbery some years back. Guy named McCall headlined it. Howard, he was in prison with this McCall. Lot of ties, huh? This money, the five thousand we recovered at your friend's house, it's clean money. Means it might not be stolen. Means too it might have been laundered and can't be traced. And Soldier, amount he's claiming Paco said there was, is a lot more than was robbed from that bank. Dirty business all the way around."

"I got this feeling," I said. "Soldier might tell a story."

"That occurred to me," Divit said. "Also occurred to me those bank officials might story some."

"A banker lie?"

"Yeah, who'd believe that?" Divit said. "Then you're saying you don't think we got cause to believe Soldier's story?"

"Not all of it. Sounds to me he's trying to work me and Leonard into this for vengeful purposes. You wouldn't want to take the word of a scum like Soldier over my word, would you?"

"You got a little record yourself," the man from the Sheriff's office said.

"Forget that," Divit said. "That's no kind of record."

The man from the sheriff's office didn't look offended. He got out his pocket knife and went to cleaning his nails.

Divit paused and looked me over. "Listen, Collins. Your friend, the war hero, Pine, he tells it like you tell it. I guess that's a better story than the one Soldier's telling. But if that money turns up, you'd let me know, wouldn't you?"

"You'd be the first," I said. "We going to trial for anything?"

"You don't end up in the middle of a slaughterhouse like that and not have to do a lot of talking. But you got a good case for self-defense. You'll be loose in a few days. Get you a pretty good ambulance chaser, and you'll do all right."

"Thanks."

"Don't thank me," Divit said. "Don't thank me for nothing."

Couple days later they let me limp down to Leonard's room. He was full of tubes and wires. Those bags they hang on those bars were all over the place, thick as fruit on trees. I hadn't expected him to look as bad as he did.

He had his head turned to me. "Hi," he said.

"Hi."

"You all right?"

"Good enough. I'm going home pretty quick. I don't know I've got enough insurance for all this."

"Man, I lay here and think about my dogs. About old Chub too. Got to considering, he bought the big one standing up for me. Well, maybe not me, but for an idea. I guess if he'd known Soldier was that nuts he'd shut up, but, you know, he maybe wasn't such a bad guy. . . . Hap, what I said about you not really being my type? Remember?"

"Yeah."

"Well, I just wanted you to know, I meant it."

I laughed.

Three days later they let me go home. I talked to Divit again, but it was a conversation not too unlike the other. He said he felt certain Soldier would get some years for a lot of things. Quite a few years. Like maybe three lifetimes. He mentioned the money again, about how if it showed up I'd keep my promise about letting him know.

I lied to him again.

I went home for a couple of days and rested, then I drove over to Leonard's. Calvin had left his spare key in the hiding spot, and I took it and went inside. All the crime scene stuff was gone and it had been cleaned up some.

Calvin had buried the dogs and nailed plywood over the busted windows. I went out to the barn and looked around. The shovel that had killed Howard and that I had used to zing Angel wasn't around. Maybe the cops called it a clue. I found a hoe, took that and limped out to the creekbank. On the way over there I noted where a lot of digging had been going on. The holes had been filled carefully and leveled off, but it didn't fool me. A country boy knows about digging and dirt, and those holes were fresh. I wondered if Divit had been here to supervise. I wondered if they had found the money. If so, I might be talking to them again and have to lie some more.

But it wasn't likely. I had an edge they didn't have. I had some idea of where it was supposed to be.

I went along the bank and found the part where the gravel had been put down. I looked around there but didn't see anyplace where she might have dug.

I guess I stayed at that for a couple of hours, looking around like that, digging a spot or two at whim, but I didn't come up with anything. I got down on the very edge of the creek and tried to think like Trudy might have thought, out here in the freezing weather with a flashlight and a shovel, trying to be quick and smart about it. I went back to the barn and took a straight path from the back door to the creekbank, walked down it to where the gravel was, then went over the edge and right up against where the water ran.

All right. Don't think about the gravel and clay except as a guide. She came here and started shining her light around. Maybe she shined it across to the other side. I looked and didn't see any dig spots, but I saw an armadillo hole in the side of the opposite bank. Roots from trees partially exposed by erosion draped over it.

I jumped the little creek and went over and looked in the hole. There was dirt not far down in the hole, so that proved the armadillo didn't live there anymore. Nothing lived there anymore. I raked back the dirt and looked inside. There were several plastic bags.

I reached in and took them out. They were those sealable bags. I stuffed my coat pockets with them, took the hoe to the barn, and went back to the house. I felt surprisingly casual. Neither the FBI nor the sheriff's department were waiting in the kitchen.

I sat down at the table and put the money on it. When I reached for one of the packets to open it, I saw the nail hole where Trudy's hand had been. I put my hand over it and centered it about where I thought the hole was.

Poor Trudy.

I opened the bags and poured out the money and counted it.

There was a little over three hundred and fifty thousand. Subtract the five thousand the authorities had, and you were still short, but not much. Trudy may have rough-counted that night, or maybe Paco palmed a little. It didn't matter.

I put a hundred thousand in one bag. It was a tight fit. I got up and got a big black trash bag out from under Leonard's sink looked through the drawers till I found a big grocery bag and some package tape and scissors. I went back to the table and sat down. I put the rest of the money in the plastic bags and put all of it, excluding that one hundred thousand, into the trash bag. I folded the bag down and around the money and made a nice compact bundle. I opened the paper bag, put the trash bag in it and folded the paper bag around it, used some package tape and the scissors to make a nice parcel.

I got up and looked around until I found a black marker. I went over and wrote in big bold letters on the package, GREEN-PEACE. I'd have to look up the rest of the address later, but seeing it written made me feel pretty good. It wasn't what Trudy had planned to do with it, but what she had planned had ultimately been in the support of things like that. I like to think she would be proud of me. After all that talk Leonard and I had given about not giving to the seals or whales, I thought there was a certain pleasant irony in it all.

The hundred thousand was for Leonard. He'd need it when he came home. If the insurance didn't pay his hospital bills, it wouldn't do him much good, high as they are, but it could give him eating money until he could go back to work.

I put the hundred thousand in my coat pocket and stuffed the package under the couch. Not exactly ace hiding places, but I figured they'd do until I got home and could do better. And besides, it had all been laundered. Who was to say it was stolen money? How was it to be proved? Greenpeace could spend that dough good as they could anyone's.

I put on Leonard's Hank Williams album, *Greatest Hits, Volume 2*, turned it up. I got one of Leonard's 40 pipes and some spare tobacco off the fireplace mantel, packed the pipe and lit it. I dragged his rocking chair out to the front porch and sat there and puffed the pipe until I remembered why I didn't smoke. I thumped out the tobacco and continued to sit there in the cold afternoon, listening to Hank Williams, occasionally flipping the record, and feeling the cold get colder.

It came to me as I sat there that Trudy, for all her blind idealism, had at least been on the right track, heading for the right station, but she got derailed.

Me, I didn't even have a station in life anymore. It was like she said, I lived from day to day and thought it was good. But she had shown me something about heart and soul again, and I knew why it was I always went with her. At the bottom of it all, she believed that things could be better than they are. That life wasn't just a game to get through. I had believed that way once, and lost it, and that's why, in spite of myself, I had always liked her coming around, no matter what it did to me. She made me believe that human beings could really make a difference. In the end, her way of doing it was as bad or worse than those she was against, but the idealism was there.

Knowing what I knew now, I could never feel exactly the way I had. I was too experienced and too practical to go back to seeing life through rose-colored glasses, or think you could figure out life's solutions with paper and a slide rule.

But to lose my idealism, to quit believing in the ability of human beings to rise above their baser instincts, was to become old and bitter and of no service to anyone, not even myself.

Idealism was a little like Venus in the daytime. There'd been a time when I could see it. But as time went on and I needed it less and wanted to pass on the responsibility, I had lost my ability to see it, to believe it. But now I thought I might see it again if I made an effort and looked hard enough.

I went inside and flipped the record for the umpteenth time, turned it all the way up, and went back and moved the rocking chair to the yard, pulled my coat around me and looked up at the sky, tried to pick out Venus before the day gave out and it got dark.

ALSO BY JOE R. LANSDALE

BAD CHILI

Hap Collins has just returned home from a gig working on an off-shore oil rig. With a new perspective on life, Hap wants to change the way he's living, and shoot the straight and narrow. That is, until the man who stole Leonard Pine's boyfriend turns up headless in a ditch and Leonard gets fingered for the murder. Hap vows to clear Leonard's name, but things only get more complicated when another body turns up—this time it's Leonard's ex.

Crime Fiction/978-0-307-45550-5

CAPTAINS OUTRAGEOUS

Hap Collins and Leonard Pine find mucho trouble, this time in Mexico, when they come face to face with a nudist mobster, his seven-foot strong-arm, an octogenarian knife-touting fisherman, and, somehow, an armadillo. When Hap Collins saves the life of his employer's daughter, he is rewarded with a Caribbean cruise, and he convinces his best friend, Leonard Pine, to come along. However, when the cruise sails on without them, stranding them in Playa del Carmen with nothing but their misfortune and Leonard's ridiculous new hat, the two quickly find themselves drawn into a vicious web of sordid violence.

Crime Fiction/978-0-307-45552-9

ALSO IN THE HAP AND LEONARD SERIES
Mucho Mojo, 978-0-307-45539-0
Rumble Tumble, 978-0-307-45551-2
The Two-Bear Mambo, 978-0-307-45549-9
Vanilla Ride, 978-0-307-45545-1

VINTAGE CRIME/BLACK LIZARD
Available at your local bookstore, or visit
www.randomhouse.com